Praise for Joseph Flynn and his novels

"Flynn is an excellent storyteller." — *Booklist*

"Flynn propels his plot with potent but flexible force."
— *Publishers Weekly*

Digger
"A mystery cloaked as cleverly as (and perhaps better than)
any John Grisham work." — *Denver Post*

"Surefooted, suspenseful and in its breathless final moments
unexpectedly heartbreaking." — *Booklist*

The Next President
"*The Next President* bears favorable comparison to such
classics as *The Best Man, Advise and Consent* and
The Manchurian Candidate."
— *Booklist*

"A thriller fast enough to read in one sitting."
— *Rocky Mountain News*

The President's Henchman (A Jim McGill Novel)
"Marvelously entertaining." — *ForeWord Magazine*

McGill's Short Cases

THREE JIM McGILL STORIES

1-3

Found Money
Lost Dog
Pins & Needles

Joseph Flynn

Stray Dog Press, Inc.
Springfield, IL
2016

ALSO By Joseph Flynn

The Jim McGill Series

The President's Henchman, A Jim McGill Novel [#1]
The Hangman's Companion, A JimMcGill Novel [#2]
The K Street Killer A JimMcGill Novel [#3]
Part 1: The Last Ballot Cast, A JimMcGill Novel [#4 Part 1]
Part 2: The Last Ballot Cast, A JimMcGill Novel [#4 Part 2]
The Devil on the Doorstep, A Jim McGill Novel [#5]
The Good Guy with a Gun, A Jim McGill Novel [#6]
The Echo of the Whip, A Jim McGill Novel [#7]
McGill's Short Cases 1-3

The Ron Ketchum Mystery Series

Nailed, A Ron Ketchum Mystery [#1]
Defiled, A Ron Ketchum Mystery Featuring John Tall Wolf [#2]
Impaled, A Ron Ketchum Mystery [#3]

The John Tall Wolf Series

Tall Man in Ray-Bans, A John Tall Wolf Novel [#1]
War Party, A John Tall Wolf Novel [#2]
Super Chief, A John Tall Wolf Novel [#3]
Smoke Signals, A John Tall Wolf Novel [#4]

The Zeke Edison Series

Kill Me Twice, A Zeke Edison Novel [#1]

Stand Alone Novels

The Concrete Inquisition
Digger
The Next President
Hot Type
Farewell Performance
Gasoline, Texas
Round Robin, A Love Story of Epic Proportions
One False Step
Blood Street Punx
Still Coming
Still Coming Expanded Edition
Hangman — A Western Novella
Pointy Teeth, Twelve Bite-Size Stories

Published by Stray Dog Press, Inc.
Springfield, IL 62704, U.S.A.

First Stray Dog Press, Inc. printing, 2014
Copyright kandrom, inc., 2016
All rights reserved

Visit the author website: *www.josephflynn.com*

Flynn, Joseph
    McGill's Short Cases 1-3 / Joseph Flynn
    106 p.
    ISBN 978-0-9908412-8-9
    ISBN ebook 978-0-9887868-3-7

Printed in the United States of America

Publisher's Note
This is a work of fiction. Names, characters, places, and incidents are either the product of the author's imagination or are used fictitiously; any resemblance to actual persons, living or dead, events, or locales is entirely coincidental.

Book design by Aha! Designs

Dedication

To my dozens of cousins. You know who you are.

Acknowledgements

Catherine and Caitie helped refine the raw texts of these stories. Any mistakes that were so wily they escaped their notice are strictly my fault.

Found Money

McGill Short Case #1

Inigo de Loyola stood on Pennsylvania Avenue outside the wrought iron fence surrounding the White House. He remained there long enough to get on the nerves of the uniformed Secret Service officers watching him. Twilight on that mild April day was about to yield to night and, though the grounds of the Executive Mansion were well lighted, the men and women charged with protecting the president knew that crazies always felt more empowered by the onset of darkness. Adding to the tension, the man outside the perimeter had his hands steepled, his head bowed and his eyes closed as if he were praying. The question was, praying for what?

Faith was a wonderful thing, but too many people who claimed to be the Almighty's personal confidants forgot all about his sixth commandment: Thou shalt not kill.

Two uniformed officers were about to head outside the fence and interview the pious figure in his hand-me-down clothes when SAC Elspeth Kendry appeared. The special agent in charge of the White House Security Detail had noticed the man while doing a routine inspection of the grounds from the roof of the mansion.

She told the uniformed captain on duty, "I'll handle this one."

"Yes, ma'am."

While following her order without quibble, the captain still positioned his two best marksmen to take the man outside the fence down, should his intentions prove more diabolical than divine. SAC Kendry was smart enough to give them a clear field of fire.

She stopped ten feet away from the man. She looked at his face. Having grown up in Beirut during dangerous times, she'd looked into the eyes of more than a few fanatics. The religiously inflamed, the politically fanatic and the mentally unhinged. She didn't get any of those vibes from this man.

As if he was not only aware of her presence — with his eyes still closed — but also knew what she was thinking, he told her, "I mean no harm. I came only to pray for the president, for her well being and for all those who live and work here."

The man opened his eyes, looked at Elspeth and introduced himself by name.

His English carried an accent. Spanish she thought, but with an overlay of Italian. It was an attractive combination when grafted onto a gentle baritone voice. The rest of him wasn't hard to take either. His hair and beard could have used barbering, but both were silver and full. His brows were as dark brown as his eyes. His nose and mouth were large but well formed.

Elspeth had also seen any number of attractive men whose souls were as vile as vomit.

She said, "I was going to say you've been here for quite a while, but if you've been praying for everyone at the White House, that's a big job."

"I have years of practice," de Loyola said.

"You're a priest?"

"I'm a Jesuit, currently without a formal assignment."

Elspeth looked at the man's clothes. Resale shop, if that. Not pressed, but still clean. No holes.

"What do you do informally, Father?"

"I minister to the poor."

"Trying to save their souls?"

"Trying to fill their bellies."

Elspeth had attended a Catholic school in Beirut.

She remembered the beatitudes.

"Blessed are the merciful," she said.

"For they will be shown mercy," de Loyola replied.

"Is there somewhere you'd like to be taken, Father?"

"Heaven, borne on the wings of angels, but I doubt that will be my fate."

He gave Elspeth a smile. Had nice teeth, too, she saw. Not common among street people.

"I am free to go?" he asked.

"Of course, Father. Go with God."

He might have taken offense, and that would have told Elspeth something.

Namely, the guy should be marked as a potential threat.

Scheduled for a more serious discussion should he make a return appearance.

But Inigo de Loyola only expanded his smile and nodded at Elspeth.

As if to say, "Good one."

Inside the building toward which Inigo de Loyola had directed his prayers, the president of the United States, Patricia Darden Grant, was having a conversation with her husband, James J. McGill, also known as the president's henchman. The two were ensconced on the leather sofa in the room known as McGill's Hideaway.

Each of them had an after-dinner drink in hand, Remy Martin cognac for the president, Jameson Irish Whiskey for McGill. Neither of them was in a hurry to down their digestifs. They were looking at the gas flame in the room's retrofitted fireplace. It was part of a project known as "The Greening of the White House."

The larger idea was to get Congress to provide low-interest loans to Americans to make their own homes as energy efficient and nonpolluting as possible.

McGill said, "It might be environmentally friendly and all that, but give me a fireplace with some crackle and the scent of wood smoke any day."

Patti said, "We have to set a good example, and you might still roast marshmallows over that flame."

McGill chuckled. "Let's do that, if you have a Girl Scout uniform at the back of your closet."

"You want to play dress up, do you? What role will you play? A forest ranger?"

"No, a wildlife biologist, flush with the victory of saving the last mating couple of … some species worth preserving."

"Something small and cute?"

"Yeah, like that. The little devils will inspire us to —"

"Roll the wrong way at just the wrong moment. Finis for the endangered species."

"You're right," McGill said, "it would probably end badly."

They skipped the marshmallows and dress-up, finished their drinks and McGill killed the gas flame with a remote control. They reclined in the darkened room with the president's back against her henchman's chest and his arms around her waist.

"We're going to have to suck it up, you and me, these next four years," Patti Grant said.

"Why's that?" McGill asked. "Because of the way you got reelected?"

The president, in a three-way race, had been elected by the last electoral ballot cast. One that had been pledged to another candidate. The fate of the nation had been decided by a college professor in Indiana. More than a few people were still upset about that.

Too bad about them, McGill thought. Nothing illegal had been done. Come to that, the president had won the popular vote. She also won a polling of the Supreme Court justices, who had voted six to three not to overturn the decision of the Electoral College.

Of course, two of the six Supreme Court votes in the president's favor had come from the chief justice and the associate justice Patricia Darden Grant had nominated not long before her reelection. Common wisdom had it that had the two previous justices survived another year, the decision would have gone the other way, five to four.

McGill had rebutted that contention by saying publicly, "Goes to show you, a higher power must have been behind the way things turned out."

Those words had struck the president to her core.

She'd very nearly died the same year the openings on the court had occurred. Her survival must have been part of the larger plan, too. It scared her to think she was just a bit player in some grand drama whose outcome was unguessable. Then she thought she'd been given more time with her husband, her stepchildren and the country she loved.

So, maybe, she was more than a bit player, and she'd better make sure she did her best for all concerned.

One more reason she told McGill, "Galia says we're going to be in for all sorts of dirty tricks."

Galia Mindel was the White House chief of staff.

It was said Galia's intelligence network had more spies than the Kremlin.

"That's okay," McGill told his wife. "That's what you've got me for."

"Galia says you could be a target, too."

McGill said, "Woe betide him who messes with me or mine."

Inigo de Loyola, Jesuit without portfolio, spent most nights sleeping on the street, as did so many of those to whom he ministered. Sharing in their deprivations built a sense of kinship and bestowed credibility. When he told the downtrodden he knew how they suffered, they saw he was telling the truth. De Loyola also hoped that his corporeal tribulations might earn him a measure of spiritual redemption.

Perhaps if he lived as long as Methuselah.

Otherwise, his only hope was divine clemency.

More likely, though, he had no real chance of deliverance. He knew his willingness to mortify the flesh was limited. Even when he spent the night outdoors, he preferred to do so in the nicest location he might find. Having arrived in Washington, D.C. two nights earlier, he found the Georgetown area to be congenial. That night, something about the white brick building on P Street near the Rock Creek Parkway called out to him.

The building was softly lighted, seemed to glow with its own grace. The susurrus of motor vehicle traffic on the parkway was almost a lullaby to his ears. There were two café tables in front of the building, but it wouldn't do to curl up on or even beneath one of them. A passing police patrol would certainly see him.

He'd be forced to move on and look for a new resting place or simply arrested. He was tired after a long day of walking, praying and fasting. He tried to remember the last time he ate, but couldn't. Tomorrow, he would have to find food.

Now, though, what he needed most was sleep. He thought he might find a peaceful niche behind the building. It looked to be very well kept, and he didn't think he'd be bothered by vermin or woodland creatures nibbling at his flesh as he slept. He smiled, thinking there was barely enough meat on his bones these days to make a meal for a mouse.

His spirit, though, was still strong. There were few things in this night or any other against which he might not give a good account of himself.

He stepped into the shadows at the near side of the building, ignoring the sign that the premises were protected by a private security company. He didn't worry about that. He had no intentions of breaking into someone else's property. He wasn't a thief.

Then there was another sign. This one warned against the grave sin of trespassing. Some assertions of evil were subject to debate, de Loyola thought. He repressed a chuckle, thinking that such debates had led him into so much difficulty with Mother Church. At the bottom of the second sign was the warning that the edict against trespass was enforced by the United States Secret Service.

Exhausted and undeterred, de Loyola made his way to the rear of the building.

Margaret "Sweetie" Sweeney was working late in the offices of McGill Investigations, Inc. She and Jim McGill had just wrapped up their first post-inaugural case, the recovery of George Washington's dentures, carved from hippopotamus ivory not wood, that had been stolen from the National Museum of Dentistry in Baltimore.

The museum was a Smithsonian affiliate and the crime normally would have been investigated by the FBI. The museum curator, Dr. Moira Moran, had sought out James J. McGill after hearing from the feds that given the ongoing threat of terrorism and the penetration of the United States by Mexican drug cartels, it might be a while before they got around to retrieving a set of false teeth, no matter what their historical value.

McGill had listened to Dr. Moran's story, made a phone call to FBI Deputy Director Byron DeWitt and asked if the bureau would mind a little help from the private sector in the matter at hand. DeWitt told McGill, "Go for it."

Dr. Moran was pleased, but she pleaded reduced government funding to the museum and asked if McGill might offer a discount on his services. Fortunately for her, he'd always had good experiences with oral health professionals and gave her half off.

McGill and Sweetie traveled to Baltimore, interviewed all relevant staffers and examined the visitors' log for the last day the dentures were known to be on the premises. Among those passing through the building was one P. James Preston of Los Angeles, California, who, a bit of research showed, was a movie producer currently pitching a project that hoped to capitalize on the film "Abraham Lincoln: Vampire Hunter."

Preston's idea for a movie was called "George Washington: America's First Zombie."

The producer had commissioned a poster for his movie pitch.

It featured a crude likeness of an undead Washington with scary-big teeth.

Seemed like a lead to McGill and Sweetie. They showed a copy of the poster to the pertinent cluster of museum staffers, with Dr.

Moran looking on, and McGill said, "Someone here took George Washington's choppers and gave them to P. James Preston. Now, either you can rat him out or we'll go to Preston and he can rat you out. As you know, the ratter gets less jail time than the rattee. Will the rat please step forward?"

Sweetie had thought that characterization was a bit harsh, but they got their man.

He hadn't even been bought off with money.

He'd been promised a part in the movie. Which doubtless would have wound up on the cutting room floor, as putting your partner in crime onscreen just might be incriminating.

Preston was arrested in L.A. in possession of the stolen oral appliance.

Washington's dentures were returned to Baltimore. McGill Investigations, Inc. was paid with a check and the gratitude of dental professionals throughout the land. Sweetie finished making her notes on the case and sent them to the firm's cloud server.

The only reason she'd stayed late at work was because her new husband, Putnam Shady, was in Omaha on business and to her great surprise, Sweetie, who always been content with her own company, now felt lonely without him.

She resolved to go home, be strong, say her rosary and go to sleep.

Before she could do any of that, she heard a man shout at the rear of the building.

Then came a yelp, followed by the sounds of a fight.

Sweetie rushed out to investigate.

Inigo de Loyola had found an agreeable resting place in the lee of a Dumpster behind the white brick building. He'd had a moment of misgiving when he spotted a low-watt light on in a ground-floor window. He pressed himself up against the wall and took a quick peek through the window. What he saw not only reassured him, it pleased him.

Inside the building was a man sleeping on a sofa, his head on a pillow, his hands resting on his abdomen. He might have been laid to eternal rest, given his absolute stillness, but morticians as a rule did not leave a smile on the lips of the dearly beloved. Nor did they provide music to accompany them on their way to judgment.

Now, being as immobile as the man inside, de Loyola could hear the strains of Beethoven's "Moonlight Sonata." *Qué exquisito.* How delightful. The Jesuit was rarely afforded a lullaby as he lay down to sleep. He ducked under the window and moved to far side of the Dumpster.

Should he begin to snore, as he'd been told he sometimes did, the trash receptacle would muffle the sound, keep the sleeper inside from being disturbed. De Loyola found a corner of the Dumpster and the building into which he might snug himself. Better yet, he detected no odor of discarded food coming from the Dumpster. The scavengers would be busy elsewhere.

Just before he lay down, the Jesuit's curiosity got the better of him. Such was the curse of the inquisitive mind. What was the trash bin used for if not unwanted portions of takeout meals? He thought perhaps he should know. As much for his own safety as anything else, he rationalized.

Another dim light, anchored in a screened fixture, provided adequate illumination for him to see what the Dumpster held. He eased the lid open, praying it would not squeak and raise an alarm from any quarter. What he found was large mounds of ... confetti?

Shredded paper, in any event. Not having a blanket to call his own, de Loyola wondered if the paper might insulate him from a night that was growing chilly. He would, of course, return the shreds of paper to their proper place in the morning. He had never been one to abuse a host's hospitality.

He leaned the lid of the Dumpster against the building and grabbed two large armloads of paper from its interior. He looked at his haul and mentally compared it to his height. Perhaps one more harvest, he thought, so he could snuggle in up to his chin.

He dug deep to make sure he'd seized a sufficient amount and saw something new. A leather valise, he thought. A carrying bag of some sort. Dark brown leather that gleamed in the soft light. Not a blemish on it. Round as if filled with … what?

Goose down perhaps? The perfect pillow to go with his new blanket.

De Loyola dug it out, marveled at the smooth suppleness of the leather. The valise was a work of truly fine craftsmanship. Much too nice to be thrown away. He pressed a hand against it, hoping to guess what it might hold. The closest he could come was another cloud of paper.

As penance for his relentless curiosity, he decided he would not look inside the valise until he rose at dawn. In the meantime, he would enjoy sleeping in his unexpectedly fine bed, hope that the soft strains of classical music would continue and ease him into slumber.

He arranged the shredded paper to his liking, positioned the bag as his pillow and was about to lie down when a large man stepped around the corner of the building. He looked at de Loyola and then the leather bag.

He yelled, "Hey!"

Then he advanced on de Loyola, a knife now in his hand.

The Jesuit knew from hard experience this was not how the police went about their business. Not in America, anyway. The expression on the man's face said de Loyola had committed a mortal sin in finding the valise and claiming it for his pillow. Now, he would pay with his life.

The man with the knife had also made a grave mistake.

He'd underestimated his opponent.

Jesuits were the traditional soldiers of the Lord.

The order's founder, Inigo's namesake, had once been a knight.

De Loyola had borne arms, too. He kicked the knife out of the man's hand. The man cried out in pain but did not halt his advance. The two of them exchanged a flurry of blows, kicks and on de Loyola's part a good bite that drew blood from the man's jowls.

That made him howl.

Then the rear door of the building opened and an angel appeared.

Or so it seemed to de Loyola.

She was tall and strong. The soft light from above made her golden hair glow. A look of righteous anger filled her eyes. De Loyola dropped to his knees and clasped his hands to his chest, thinking judgment was near. The man who had attacked him turned and ran.

It was then the Jesuit noticed the angel had a gun in her hand.

Being called away from family and home had become a far less frequent occurrence for McGill since he'd opened his private business. It had happened frequently during his early years as a Chicago cop. Wondering if he'd come home alive and unhurt had contributed to the fears of his first wife, Carolyn, that eventually led to their divorce.

McGill was not without sympathy for Carolyn, but the role of protector was in his blood. He and Carolyn made their separation as free of recrimination as possible, using the same lawyer, for the sake of their children, Abbie, Kenny and Caitie.

The irony was, not long after the dissolution of their marriage, McGill made the jump in rank to lieutenant and then captain. He became an administrator, leaving street work behind. After putting in his twenty years with the CPD and receiving his master's degree in criminal justice administration, he became chief of police in the gilded North Shore suburb of Winnetka, Illinois.

Violent crime was rare indeed there, until Andrew Hudson Grant, billionaire philanthropist and first husband of Patricia Darden Grant, was murdered by an antiabortion extremist. McGill arrested the culprit within twenty-four hours.

Wound up marrying the woman who became the first female president.

Talk about things that were meant to be.

Leaving the White House with Secret Service Special Agent Deke Ky and Leo Levy, his personal driver, McGill felt almost young again. He was running out into the dark of night, answering Sweetie's call to come see what she'd caught lurking out back of their office.

Knowing his longtime partner in law enforcement, the detainee might be anyone from an angel with a dirty face to R.W. Fisher, the FBI's most wanted man, formerly known as public enemy number one. Sweetie was an all-purpose ex-cop.

When McGill, Deke and Leo hurried into the offices on P Street each of them had his gun in hand. All of them were brought up short by a sign affixed to the door of McGill's office.

Don't knock. Confession in Progress.

Deke, ever the skeptic, said, "Could be a fake-out."

Leo said, "Don't think so. Margaret could get O.J. to 'fess up."

A contention yet to be proved, but one McGill thought possible.

He said, "Let's give it a minute. Deke, you cover the back of the building. Leo, you take the front."

"Chase the bad guy, if he gets into his wheels?" Leo asked.

Leo had been a NASCAR driver before going to work for McGill.

McGill nodded.

Then he had to wait five minutes before the door to his office opened.

Sweetie smiled at him. Looked peaceful. Radiant, even.

"You're okay?" he asked. "You look okay."

"Fresh from confession," she said.

That backed McGill up a step. Sweetie had given her confession, hadn't taken one? That had to mean … "You grabbed a priest?"

Sweetie gestured someone forward. A distinguished-looking man in resale shop clothing stepped forward. He looked at McGill, nodded and smiled.

McGill half-expected to receive a blessing.

Sweetie introduced the two men.

McGill said, "You were named for a saint?"

"So many of us are," de Loyola said. "You yourself, for example."

"Got me there," McGill admitted. "If not to the same extent as you."

Sweetie said, "Father de Loyola was praying for you earlier tonight, Jim."

McGill understood his role now. He was Sweetie's foil.

The priest's, too.

"With any particular result?" he asked de Loyola.

"As it happens, I chose to make my bed behind your building tonight."

"Purely by circumstance," McGill said.

"That or divine guidance, depending on your degree of faith."

"Fair enough," McGill said. "Now, can we get to the good part?"

Sweetie said, "Father de Loyola found a leather bag left in the Dumpster out back. In it, there was a note addressed to you by name. The note's message was 'paid in full.' There was also a half-million dollars in the bag."

McGill stepped past Sweetie and de Loyola. Took the seat behind his desk. Thought about the implications of the discovery. Patti had warned him that dirty tricks would be coming. The money might have traces of drug residue on it. It might be the proceeds of a robbery. Or it might be counterfeit. It had to be incriminating in some way.

Then someone would be alerted to the money's existence.

Newsies, cops or both.

Wouldn't that be fun for Patti at the start of her second term?

De Loyola took a step toward McGill.

He said, "I can see you are troubled, sir. If it would be of any help to you, I would like to claim this money as my own."

McGill called the feds and the local cops. SAC Elspeth Kendry, as the Secret Service had the responsibility of investigating counterfeit money, if that was what it was. Captain Rockelle Bullard of the Metro PD was called to investigate the assault of Father de Loyola, and to look into the matter of making sure he was who he claimed to be.

For just a moment, Sweetie looked disconcerted by the idea

that she might have bared her soul to a con-man. She shook off her doubt. She knew better than to be taken in on a matter of faith. De Loyola was the real thing, a priest.

On the outs with the church hierarchy, as he freely admitted.

The Jesuit had been taken to George Washington University Hospital to be given a physical examination, in case he'd bitten into someone toxic. He'd be kept overnight for observation and in the morning Elspeth and Rockelle would decide if he should be detained further.

"What about his claim on the money?" the Metro police captain asked McGill.

"He found it. I don't want it," McGill said. "If you want to be mean about things, I suppose you could consult legal counsel. Lawyers' fees could eat up the whole amount in short order."

Sweetie shook her head. "You know what? I say not only is the money real, it won't have any traces of drugs on it and it won't have come from any heist. Won't be funny money either."

"Your rationale being?" McGill asked.

"If the money was connected to any obvious criminal activity, it would be that much harder for anyone to believe you were connected to it. If it's clean, it'd be easier for people to accept you were taking a kickback for something. You'd deny it, but that would only reinforce doubts."

Elspeth nodded. "I can buy that."

"Me, too," Rockelle said. "If we're right, you got somebody smart after you."

McGill shook his head. He didn't need this crap.

"Turning the money in to the police isn't enough to clear me?" he asked.

Sweetie said, "For us, sure. People who don't like you could say you just got cold feet."

McGill asked, "When is Putnam getting back to town?"

Putnam Shady had acted as McGill's lawyer at a Congressional hearing.

"I'll call him," Sweetie said. "He'll be on the first plane."

"Thank you." McGill got to his feet. "If no one wants to arrest me, I'm going home."

He needed to talk to Patti. Galia, too.

Start planning the counteroffensive.

That gave McGill an idea. He sat down again.

He asked Sweetie, "You think you could see who comes to pick up the trash in the morning? Whoever scripted this plan needs someone to discover the ill-gotten cash and raise a ruckus."

Sweetie nodded. She was on McGill's wavelength as usual.

She said, "After the pickup man sees the money is gone, he can't say, 'Hey look what I found out behind Jim McGill's office.' So I can follow him back to whoever hired him."

"With a little help from the guys," McGill said. He turned to Deke and Leo, "You guys up for that?"

Deke nodded. Leo gave a thumbs up.

Rockelle Bullard looked at McGill and Sweetie. "If you two will search your memories just a little bit, I'm sure you'll remember the police do this sort of thing, too. In fact, most folks would say we should do it first."

McGill sympathized. In Rockelle's place, he'd feel the same way.

"It's your call, Captain. But then you and your detectives will own what you find, and whatever political heat might come with it. That might not be any fun at all. If you start out the way we discussed, seeing who attacked the good father, you'll be close enough for us to hand off the rest to you, if that's what you want. On the other hand, maybe SAC Kendry might want to carry the load."

Elspeth, more wily than her local law enforcement colleague, knew better.

She said, "Pardon me, but did anyone hear me ask for any favors?"

Rockelle caught Elspeth's drift and needed no further dissuasion.

"Yeah, maybe I'll leave things with you for the time being, Mr. McGill," she said. "But we'll all keep in touch, right?"

"Absolutely," McGill said.

***

Galia Mindel, the White House chief of staff, sat before the makeup mirror in the master bathroom of her Dumbarton Oaks home. She turned her head to the right and to the left, keeping an eye cocked on her reflection. She pulled her hair back and studied the line it made across her forehead. Finally, she swung a second mirror out from its wall mount and examined the crown of her head.

Sighing in relief, she thought all strands were present and accounted for, and none of them had gone gray. Thank God, she'd inherited her mother's permacolor brunette gene — even if she liked to touch it up with artificial highlights — and had dodged her father's family history of alopecia. It had afflicted even poor Aunt Sophie and Aunt Daphna. With the stress Galia had been under since the president's second inauguration, she felt it was a wonder that she had any hair at all.

The political battles surrounding the Electoral College vote that had put Patricia Darden Grant back in the Oval Office had been ferocious. The Supreme Court decision upholding the president's re-election had come from a clear majority, but Galia had hoped for 7-2 or 8-1 in favor. Instead, she saw there was still a conservative rump on the court, and their dissenting opinion had been scathing. All but accusing the majority of stealing the election for the president.

Galia had been tempted to resign her position and come right out and tell those three old reactionaries, "Hey, fuck you, too." Maybe even, "Hurry up and die already so we can put three more women on the bench." The president had talked her out of such rash behavior.

Not that they hadn't laughed about the idea in private.

In the end, Galia had let herself be flattered that she was irreplaceable.

The president had to have her.

At such a cost, though. Oy! She'd lost thirty-two pounds the past three months. She would never have imagined her metabolism was still capable of such a thing. It was only in the past three weeks the president had insisted that Galia adopt the presidential diet — leaves and twigs, as the chief of staff had always thought of it — and start exercising with the president, too.

My God! Getting up before the sun had risen over Iceland. Taking weights in hand. Curling her arms. Raising them above her shoulders. Lunging forward like some clumsy species of biped brushed aside by evolution as a nonstarter. The best she could say about the whole grueling experience was …

It was working. Not only had her limbs, middle and derriere been shorn of layers of fat, they were reforming into the most pleasant shapes. Sleek planes and arcs. Tone, the president had called the development. Who knew such things were even possible for a woman her age?

Between the emotional giddiness and the deep muscular pain of her makeover, she almost forgot to worry. When she did worry, the concern was met by a new response. She was going to kick somebody's ass. She'd always felt that way emotionally, of course. Getting even was a trait inherited from both her parents. But now she felt she could really go out and do physical damage to an enemy.

After swearing Galia to secrecy, the president had even started to show her a move or two from James J. McGill's Dark Alley system of self-defense.

Other than insuring a positive legacy for the president and keeping the ship of state from foundering on the rocks of True South obstructionism, the only thing that really worried Galia now was her face. It had lost suet, too, and there were bags under her eyes and drapes of skin on her cheeks. But there was no facial Pilates to tone those things up.

The president had said, "Try smiling more."

After seeing Galia force a smile, Patti Grant had said, "We'll think of something."

What Galia was thinking, as she applied her mask of Olay Total Effects Night Firming Cream, was a facelift. She'd have to take time off for the procedure and recovery. When she returned everyone in the White House Press Room would see the change immediately. If even one of them dared to laugh at her, she would —

Answer the bathroom phone before it finished its first ring.

Only the president had the number that rang in her bathroom. And now apparently her husband, too.

James J. McGill told her, "Sorry about the hour, Galia. But something's come up. Can you come right over to the Residence?"

Inigo de Loyola looked at Agnes Cudahy, the nurse taking his pulse in the private hospital room where he'd been placed, and told her, "I am ashamed."

Professional that she was, Agnes collected and recorded her data before asking, "Ashamed of what?"

"Being warm, cleanly clothed and receiving medical attention when there are so many who lack all these things."

Agnes nodded. "President Kennedy told us life isn't fair."

She'd been a young girl when Kennedy was president, still remembered him as an impossibly handsome man. There hadn't been a president who came anywhere near him for glamour, until Patti Grant had been elected. Agnes was now two weeks away from retirement.

"A rather obvious observation," de Loyola said. "But what did this president of yours do about the inequities he saw?"

"Started the Peace Corps," Agnes said.

"That was him?"

Agnes nodded.

"I stand humbled."

Truth was, the Jesuit lay in a hospital bed. He was perfectly able to sit or stand, walk or even run. But the bed was so comfortable. He'd almost forgotten the pleasure of lying on a firm mattress with clean sheets. And the pillows, *Madre de Dios*. Agnes had found him two stuffed with goose down. The ones that had come with the bed were foam. He hadn't murmured a word of complaint about that, but his face must have shown disappointment. Agnes had fetched these marvelous replacements.

Feeling guilty, he said, "I should be in a ward with other patients. Souls to whom I might offer consolation to the best of my humble abilities."

It had pleased de Loyola deeply to be able to hear Margaret Sweeney's confession.

Agnes told him, "Father, we don't have wards in this hospital."

"No?"

"No. If you'd like, I'll have the hospital chaplain stop by in the morning. Maybe he'll have some chores you can help him with."

De Loyola smiled, "Thank you. You are very kind."

"And you are in good health, though borderline malnourished. I'm going to bring you a carton of chocolate milk. Drink it and then enjoy a good night's sleep. Eat the breakfast you'll be given. There are no commandments against any of that."

Nurse Agnes was on theologically firm ground there, the Jesuit thought.

He did as he was told. Drank the milk. Snuggled into the goose down pillows.

Thanked the Lord for all the comforts afforded to him that night.

Promised to find a way to express his gratitude by helping others. As he drifted off to sleep, he thought that being allowed to keep the money he had found would help him go a long way toward helping others. What were the chances that would happen?

Very slight indeed, he felt.

But Agnes had given him an idea with her mention of the Peace Corps.

Maybe he could start a Street Corps.

Uplift all those without a home to call their own.

After Sheryl Kimbrough had cast the electoral vote that returned Patricia Darden Grant to the White House and the Supreme Court had confirmed the validity of one person deciding a presidential election, the president decided she wanted a room in the Executive Mansion that would be her counterpart to McGill's Hideaway.

That room was in the northeast corner of the ground floor.

The space's original purpose was to act as a laundry room for John Adams. Millard Fillmore's wife, Abigail, repurposed it as a library. The library was used to hold teas in the 1950s. The Kennedys had it recreated as a Federal Style parlor.

Patti Grant had it redone as the "world's ultimate reading room." To that end, she asked that any publication on the planet — including those intended by foreign governments to be kept secret — be available to her in the library. As the theft of data files was far easier to manage than that of printed books, the president did much of her reading on e-readers. Given the sensitivity of perusing other people's secrets, the walls, ceiling and floor of the room were reinforced with the best available anti-snooping technology.

Even the curtains on the windows did more than block outside light.

There were also locks on the doors. Not unheard of in the White House but rare in a place where Secret Service agents were never more than a cry for help away. When the door to the library was locked, only five people had the means to open it: the president, Vice President Jean Morrissey, Chief of Staff Galia Mindel, SAC Elspeth Kendry and James J. McGill.

McGill and Galia were in the room with the president. Vice President Morrissey was in her home state of Minnesota and Elspeth Kendry had been told do not disturb. If the president absolutely had to be reached, her personal secretary, Edwina Byington, was allowed to buzz the phone extension.

By now, though, Edwina would have been in bed for hours.

McGill told Patti and Galia the story of what had rousted him out of the White House on what he'd expected to be a quiet night at home.

The president deferred to her chief of staff to be the first to respond.

Galia said, "This was definitely intended to be a smear. In a way, it's similar to what happened to the Clintons in their first term with the so-called White Water scandal. You get the press worked up with accusations of wrongdoing. Political enemies start yelling for an independent prosecutor. All the administration's energy goes into playing defense. None is left for its own priorities."

Patti nodded. She turned to her husband for his view on the matter.

McGill said, "No point sticking around another four years just to play someone else's game."

"I agree," the president said. "Having Sweetie, Deke and Leo find out who's behind this is important. We have to know who we're fighting here."

Galia said, "We have to do more than that." The chief of staff knew all the new security features of the library. She felt free to express herself candidly. "We have to kick them in the balls."

McGill smiled. The two women saw he had something in mind.

"Jim?" the president asked.

He had a question for the chief of staff. "Does Ellie Booker still work for WorldWide News?"

"She has a first-look agreement with them for any project she might want to do," Galia said.

McGill thought the chief of staff must have a room in her own house akin to the one in which they currently sat. The place where she read reports from her spies all over town and across the world. That had to be how she knew the TV producer's employment status.

McGill needed to learn what else Galia knew about Ms. Booker.

"So she's making money strictly on the chance she might come up with a bright idea?"

"Yes. If Hugh Collier likes a project she wants to do, he gets first crack at it. If it's not for him, or he doesn't want to pay top dollar, she can take it elsewhere."

"Is there any personal loyalty between the two of them?"

Galia said, "I don't see either of them thinking in those terms."

"Good."

"What are you getting at, Jim?" Patti asked.

"The setup of planting the money behind my office depends on setting off a big media storm. Now, Sweetie and the guys can follow the trail their way, but another way to find out what we want to know is to discover who in the media plans to make their reputation with a scoop on my being corrupt. I was thinking if anyone could point us in the right direction, it would be Ellie Booker."

Galia said, "But you didn't take her case when she came to you."

Ellie Booker had wanted McGill to help clear her of responsibility in the death of Reverend Burke Godfrey. Politically, that was a nonstarter. McGill, however, had extended the producer the courtesy of meeting with her.

He said, "No, I didn't. But I was honest with her. Respectful. And when I told her that I'd sink Sir Edbert Bickford's ship if necessary, there was a gleam in her eye."

"You always were a charmer," Patti said.

Galia wasn't going to say so aloud, but she had to agree.

Instead of paying McGill a compliment, she asked him, "So you'll try to use Ellie Booker to find out who this particular political enemy is?"

"Not just find him," McGill said. "Return his money to him. Let him explain the bag of cash that will be found on *his* doorstep."

The president beamed at her husband.

"A story you'll present gift wrapped to Ms. Booker."

"Yeah," McGill said. "That works nicely, doesn't it?"

"Is there anything else you'll need to do?" Galia asked.

It was her job to make sure McGill's scheming didn't backfire.

Cause an unintended scandal for the president.

McGill admitted, "There is one thing."

"What's that?" Patti asked.

"I'll have to corrupt a priest."

Alone in the presidential bedroom an hour later, just snuggling because McGill would be working through the night, Patti said, "This is all my fault, Jim."

He nodded, "I blame you entirely."

McGill made sure to wrap his arms around his wife and kiss her before she could give him an elbow to the ribs.

Continuing, he said, "If you mean doing just enough to win reelection, you have to share responsibility with Galia, your entire campaign staff, the tens of millions of Americans who voted for you, six members of the Supreme Court who said okey-dokey and me for encouraging you to run the first time."

"You forgot Sheryl Kimbrough," Patti said.

McGill released his wife from his embrace and slapped his head.

"Of course, the journalism prof at Indiana University. The final elector to have her say."

"Taking your point of view, I'm in good company, but I still feel responsible," Patti said.

"I appreciate your concern, but if you look at it a bit more closely, the creeps, whoever they might be, are insulting me."

"What do you mean?"

"Well, look at what they did. Tried to make me look sleazy, corrupt and maybe criminal by taking half-a-million dirty dollars. What would that amount of money represent to you? A pittance."

Philanthropist Andrew Hudson Grant had left his widow billions.

"But to me five hundred grand is a hefty chunk of money," McGill said.

"What, the bad guys don't think I'll share with you?" Patti asked.

"That's beside the point. They'll say my male ego demanded that I grab all the money I could to have and to hold in my own name. Hence the reason I crossed ethical lines at the very least."

The president drew her head back and regarded her husband.

"Nobody who knows you would ever think that."

"That's true. If you ever kick me to the curb, I still have a going business, two police pensions and hold the title to a perfectly nice house back in Evanston, Illinois. But none of that matters because the people behind this scheme will do their best to paint a whole new me to the public. It would not only taint your administration, it would hurt Abbie, Kenny and Caitie."

McGill had, for the most part, kept his children out of the glare of the president's media coverage. But if he was smeared, the kids and McGill's ex-wife, Carolyn, would inevitably be dragged into the spotlight. Patti's face hardened as she digested her husband's surmise.

"You're right," she said. "We can't have any of that. You'd better get going."

They'd been lucky enough to reach Ellie Booker.

She was editing film footage for some unspecified project.

Had agreed to meet McGill at one a.m.

McGill stood and looked at his wife.

"We'll find some time for ourselves soon?"

Patti told him, "I'll have Edwina block out a whole afternoon for us. How's that?"

McGill beamed.

Not even visiting heads of state got that much of the president's day.

McGill sat opposite Ellie Booker with a battered metal desk between them. Shelves of videotape lined the walls. There wasn't so much as a plastic daffodil in a dimestore vase to relieve the oppressive atmosphere of the small room. The overhead fluorescent lights made the obviously fatigued TV news producer look like she'd just stepped off the set of a slasher movie.

"Love what you've done with the place," McGill said.

Ellie gave him a thin smile.

"I'm paying the rent here, not WorldWide News."

"But you have a first-look deal with Hugh Collier."

Ellie opened her mouth to ask a question. Like, "How the hell did you know that?" But she remembered the kind of connections McGill must have, being married to the president. She didn't think McGill had sicced some government agency on her, but Galia Mindel certainly tracked all real and potential enemies of the president. One-stop shopping for McGill when he wanted the lowdown on someone like her.

"Yes, I do," she told McGill, "but I'm a thrifty girl. That's how I keep my independence."

He said, "Very wise."

"So what do you want?" Ellie asked.

"Information. Now's the time to say you can't help me, if you want to."

Ellie laughed and actual points of color appeared on her high cheekbones.

"I do like to even accounts, but for someone like you to show up here in the middle of the night, I'll bet you have something interesting to tell me."

"Just that I want to give you a scoop." He looked around the room. "One that might let you indulge in just a bit more creature comfort."

"Information, huh? You want me to sell someone out."

"I do. I want to know who in the Washington and New York media ..." A thought occurred to McGill. "Let's add London to that list. Who in that media axis might have been gossiping about nailing me with a screaming exposé?"

Ellie Booker blinked twice. That was all it took for McGill to see she didn't know. Must have been working too hard on her own project to come up for air.

"You haven't heard?" he said. "I'm sorry I bothered you."

He started to get up when Ellie raised her hand.

"Wait, wait, wait. You wouldn't have come here expecting me to tell you something like that without having something good to offer in return. Is your *scoop* really that compelling?"

McGill settled back into his chair. He was glad he'd read Ellie at least halfway right.

"It is, but if you don't have the information I need ..."

"If someone's looking to stick it to you and has been dumb enough to blab about it, I can find out quick."

"What if the person is a friend of yours?"

Ellie smiled broadly. McGill was pleased to see she didn't have fangs.

"I don't have any friends," she said. "Not the kind that would get in the way of a good story. So you want to tell me what I should look for and how it helps me?"

McGill told her.

Then he cautioned, "Don't just hand me someone you dislike. I'll know if it's who I want."

"You've got someone else looking, too."

"I do."

"But I'm the only one who gets to go with the story."

"It will be yours exclusively," McGill said.

Inigo de Loyola was awakened by a soft knock at his hospital room door. He knew it wasn't Agnes or any of the other nurses. The hospital was their domain. They didn't need to knock to visit patients. The necessity of caring for the ailing was their admission ticket.

With a bit of trepidation in his voice, de Loyola said, "Come in."

He knew you had to be careful not to extend an invitation to the devil.

At this hour, though, he thought even Satan must be resting.

So who could …

He saw James J. McGill slip into his room and close the door behind him. McGill held a bag in his hand. De Loyola had gained from talking to Agnes and other hospital staffers some measure of the men who had delivered him to the hospital. They were the henchmen of the man called the president's henchman.

De Loyola had rather liked that sobriquet.

It put him in mind of a knight errant. Someone called upon when the usual instruments of power proved inadequate to surmount a challenge. A man of unusual resources. Willing to commit a sin or two if necessary, repent and accept his penance without complaint.

McGill drew a chair up to the side of the bed and said, "I'm sorry to disturb you, Father."

"And yet you have. For good reason, no doubt."

"Yes, for good reason. How are you feeling?"

De Loyola took a moment to assess. "Better than if I'd spent the night on cold concrete. But there is a hollow ache in my middle. I've not supped for a day or two."

McGill raised the white bag he'd brought with him into de Loyola's view.

"Four sandwiches from the White House kitchen: ham, chicken, roast beef and, if you don't eat meat, fried onions and roasted tomatoes."

De Loyola raised the head of his bed; Agnes had showed him how.

He said to McGill, "I'll take them all. May I start with the onions and tomatoes while I listen to your proposition?"

McGill gave the sandwich to the priest. Poured him a glass of water from the pitcher on the stand next to the bed. He didn't ask how the priest knew he wanted something. A visit at that hour made it obvious.

He was pleased to see de Loyola smile as he took his first bite.

De Loyola took his stole out of the drawer of the night stand on the far side of his bed, pressed it to his lips and draped it over his shoulders. He looked at McGill and smiled, saying, "Yours will not be the first confession I've heard from a hospital bed. My labors have taken me to war zones."

"As a military chaplain?" McGill asked.

"That and a guerrilla. My politics might not be the same as yours."

"I'm for what's right for the little guy, Father."

De Loyola gave McGill his blessing then and there.

"We are compadres," the Jesuit said. "Now tell me how you might have offended God."

After a moment's hesitation, McGill told de Loyola of his roles in the deaths of John Patrick Granby and Damon Todd.

"I don't see how I could have acted differently in either case, Father, but I'd never taken anyone's life before and then I was responsible for the deaths of two men in a short period of time. Sometimes I can sleep through the night without a problem; other times I can't sleep at all."

To McGill's surprise, de Loyola responded, "I know how you feel. I know *just* how you feel. We are commanded by God not to kill. But we are also instructed that there is no greater love than laying down one's life for another. Sometimes we may risk our lives for those of others, survive that trial and cause the death of the source of menace."

De Loyola rubbed his bearded chin as his eyes filled with a painful memory.

"Such situations never allow time for reflection. We must act without hesitation. Yet we must be *sure* the danger is real." The priest's eyes now focused on McGill. "Here you have the advantage of me. In the situations you describe, you truly had no choice. In one case, it would have been a moral offense had you remained passive, and in the other you would have been acquiescing to your own murder.

"You are without sin in these matters, my friend. You owe no penance as such. What you might do to salve your pain is to look for more chances to ease the suffering of others."

De Loyola was about to remove his stole when McGill asked him to let it be.

"Your confession is not finished?" the priest asked.

"We need to talk about the sins I'm going to commit," McGill said.

The Jesuit told him, "Confession is not a prospective sacrament. You cannot bank absolution."

"I'm not asking for forgiveness now, Father. I'm looking for an accomplice."

De Loyola exhibited surprise. Then he smiled broadly.

"We are indeed brothers-in-arms," the priest said.

McGill told him, "The money you found and asked for, Father? I'm afraid you can't have it, but I know where you can get a substantial amount. Maybe even an ongoing source of funds, if you want to use it for a good cause."

De Loyola thought of his idea for the Street Corps. Having someone underwrite that plan would be manna from heaven. He and this henchman truly shared many bonds. The Jesuit, as his superiors in the hierarchy well knew, was not beyond sinning.

He would repent, of course.

Do his penance without complaint.

"What do you need, sir?" he asked McGill.

"The first thing is your vow of silence."

Draped in his stole, the priest steepled his hands. "The seal of confession is inviolable."

Dikki Missirian, the owner of the building in which McGill Investigations, Inc. had its offices, was usually the first to arrive at the Georgetown address in the morning. Mr. McGill and Margaret Sweeney normally arrived at nine a.m., as did the staff at the accounting firm of Wentworth & Willoughby on the second floor. Max Lucey, the owner and chief recording engineer of A-Sharp Sound on the ground floor, came and went at all hours, but his days usually started close to the lunch hour.

So when Dikki arrived at six-fifteen a.m., a half-hour before sunrise, he was surprised to be greeted by Max. Dikki's office was also on the ground floor, a small space tucked under the building's staircase.

"Good morning, Max. You were working late?"

The sound engineer nodded. "Yeah, I was. Listening to the final mix of a new blues album. Wanted to make sure I have all the sound levels right. Dikki, did any of the building's alarms get set off last night?"

If something had been amiss, the building owner would have

been notified by either his private security firm or the Secret Service. He looked disturbed by Max's question.

"No, I received no calls. Did you hear something?"

Max said, "No, I guess not. I stretched out on the sofa in my office. Fell asleep listening to Beethoven and started dreaming. Thought I heard a scuffle out back."

"Scuffle?"

"Fight. Guys duking it out. Didn't last long. I got up to use the john later and took a peek out the back door. Didn't see anything."

Dikki started to relax. Max yawned and stretched.

"Funny thing was," the sound engineer said, "when I lay down again I thought I heard people climbing the stairs. But you've got alarms on W&W, right?"

"Yes, of course," Dikki said.

"That's what I thought. And the Secret Service takes care of Mr. McGill's space. So I went back to sleep."

The two men paused to consider the situation. Four years earlier, a psychotic psychiatrist had broken into Jim McGill's office and tried to kill him. The creep had knocked Dikki out in his little office. People in the building had been on edge for some time after that. But years went by with nothing unusual happening … you wrote it off as a once in a lifetime thing.

Right?

Max and Dikki were trying to do just that.

The sound engineer asked his landlord, "You want to hear a sample of the new album?"

Dikki was a blues fan. He'd never heard the music before arriving in the United States from Armenia, but loved it from the first plaintive note to reach his ears. He attributed this to his natal country's heartbreaking history of being conquered — fourteen times in two centuries — suffering an attempt at genocide at the beginning of the twentieth century and enduring violent protests against the new, independent government a hundred years later.

He could relate to music that sang of people's sorrows.

The two men were heading toward Max's sound board in the

recording studio when they saw the trash-hauling truck go by the window that looked out on the alley.

Morning pickup.

Only the usual guy wasn't behind the wheel.

Sweetie watched the back of Dikki Missirian's building. She had set up a vantage point on the roof of the neighboring building. She saw the driver of the trash-hauling truck bring his vehicle to a stop. He got out of the cab and looked around, as if to see if anyone might be watching him. Hardly the usual behavior for someone in his line of work.

Trash collectors didn't tend to be self-conscious about doing their jobs.

People scheming against the president's husband had more reason to be nervous.

The man who got out of the truck didn't spot Sweetie. She wore dark clothes and a navy blue stocking cap to cover her blonde hair. The cell phone in the cargo pocket on her right leg vibrated twice, went still and then vibrated twice more. Deke and Leo had just checked in.

Their message was: The man who got out of the truck had company, someone sitting nearby in another vehicle. Leo was positioned to follow the second party. Sweetie raised her Canon Elph LT camera to her eye. There was enough light in the brightening sky to shoot without a flash. She took her first shot of the driver as he approached the Dumpster behind Dikki's building.

Got the guy's face full on.

What someone in his line of work should have done was push the wheeled Dumpster out behind his rear-loader truck. Align the Dumpster with his cart-lifter. Have the machinery dump the load and set the trash bin back on the ground to be returned to its point of origin.

There was no need to inspect the trash that got dumped.

Unless, of course, you expected to find something.

Sweetie's camera silently captured the efforts of the man below to have his Eureka moment. His first few armloads of shredded paper were taken out of the Dumpster in a methodical fashion. Grabbed and stacked nearby and neatly, making the return of the refuse to the container quick and easy.

As the man plumbed deeper into the Dumpster without result, though, he became agitated. He hurled the waste about helter-skelter. Events weren't following the script he'd been given and he wasn't comfortable improvising. The man leaned over the Dumpster, the upper half of his body descending into the trash receptacle. He swung an arm back and forth as if stirring a giant pot of soup.

He soon emerged, stepped back from the Dumpster and gave it a kick.

He took a cell phone from his pocket and hit a single button.

Sweetie listened in on the man's call with a small device called a Signal Magnet. SigMag, as it was called in the government snooping trade. She wasn't supposed to have one; only federal agents were authorized to carry the device. Captain Welborn Yates of the United States Air Force Office of Special Investigations was a federal agent. He worked out of the White House on detached duty to the president. He had a SigMag and had been looking the other way when Jim McGill borrowed it.

The device could record the calls it snooped, but that would create a record of its use.

Neither McGill nor Sweetie wanted that.

Relying on Sweetie's memory would do for their purposes.

McGill stood in front of Rockelle Bullard's house on W Street in North West Washington. The metro police captain opened the trunk of her meticulously washed and waxed ice blue Chevy Impala, vintage 1965. McGill gave the vehicle a smile of appreciation.

"Beautiful ride, Captain," McGill told her.

"Thank you."

Rockelle swore that she didn't mind being awakened early but anyone could see she had a grump on. SAC Elspeth Kendry saw it, easily. McGill had put her out of sorts, too. With Deke Ky and Leo Levy off doing other tasks for McGill, she had to act as his bullet-catcher.

Not that she minded his company. He was smart, honest and almost as funny as he thought he was. Altogether more human than someone in his position needed to be. But while she was out on the street making sure the president didn't get widowed a second time, the paperwork generated by the administrative side of her job piled up.

She hated doing any paperwork.

Facing a backlog really made her crazy.

Rockelle pointed to the cardboard box inside her trunk.

"Bag's in the box," she said. "Money's in the bag."

McGill was impressed. He understood the captain hadn't been reckless leaving a half-million dollars parked at the curb. She knew nobody in her neighborhood, and probably the whole town, would mess with her car. That was why she didn't have to put the classic gem in a garage.

It also told McGill the money had never been logged in with the Metro PD.

Rockelle Bullard had anticipated correctly that McGill might need the cash.

He grabbed the box.

Told Rockelle she need not concern herself about the money any further.

"Because you're not going to play finders-keepers."

"Right," McGill had said.

He put the box in the trunk of his turbocharged Chevy, light years ahead of Rockelle's car in technology, safety and power. Nowhere near it in breathless cool. Maybe someday Detroit would put it all together.

McGill asked, "When the time's right, you want me to tell you what happened?"

Rockelle shook her head. "I'd just as soon not know."

McGill gave her a salute and left with Elspeth at the wheel.

Max Lucey and Dikki Missirian stood in front of Dikki's building on P Street when the trash-hauling truck barreled out of the alley, slowed just long enough to see there was no approaching cross-traffic and made a hard right turn, the driver gunning the engine for all it was worth. It was almost comical watching the big, clumsy vehicle trying to gain speed. Once it got going, though, it was going to need as much room as a jumbo jet to come to a stop. Heaven help anything that got in its way.

The truck was halfway down the block when a red Mini Cooper pulled out of a parking space, made a U-turn on the narrow street and charged after the truck. Tailgated the larger vehicle so close it looked like an automotive hemorrhoid.

"What the hell is going on?" Max Lucey asked.

He and Dikki stepped out into the street.

Dikki took out his mobile phone ready to record any further lunacy.

Sure enough, down the block, parked on the near side of the street, a stretch Cadillac pulled out and joined the caravan, proceeding more sedately than the Mini Cooper and the truck.

Dikki videoed the Cadillac's departure. The garbage truck and Mini Cooper had turned left at 26th Street; the Caddy turned right. Maybe it had just happened to be going the same way for a short distance. Max and Dikki looked at each other. Asked the question without saying a word.

Just a coincidence, the Caddy pulling out right after the other two vehicles passed by?

No way.

Max said, "Make sure to keep that video."

Dikki replied, "Yes, of course."

Leo Levy and Deke Ky kept track of the trash-hauling truck

the modern way. Not tailing it from behind. Watching it from in front, using a rear-facing video camera. Many newer model cars had such cameras to aid drivers in parking their cars in tight spaces. Leo had modified the camera in his car to watch vehicles traveling behind him. The lens could be tilted up or down to adjust to the height of the target vehicle.

The video captured by the camera was displayed on a monitor set into Leo's dashboard.

Leo, of course, kept his eyes on the road. Even a pro had to watch where he was going.

But Deke, riding shotgun, said, "That guy looks like his day isn't starting out the way he'd hoped. Whoops! Did you see that?"

"Caught it in my mirror," Leo said.

A tiny red car that they hadn't even known was behind the truck made a screeching right turn onto a side street. It disappeared in seconds. Neither Deke nor Leo worried about it.

"A reporter," Leo said.

"Just lost his big story," Deke added.

By now, the truck was starting to crowd Leo's rear bumper. He smoothly pulled into an open space at the curb. The truck roared past, the driver not having needed to honk his horn. Leo pulled back into the near lane.

The truck turned a corner two blocks up. Leo didn't hurry to catch up. They already had an excellent idea of where it was heading. Sweetie had e-mailed them the photos she'd taken of the truck driver. Deke had forwarded them to the White House Security Detail. A colleague there started his check of the man's identity by running the image of his face against those of visitors who had taken the White House tour during the past twelve months. Found him among the tourists passing through two weeks after the president's second inauguration.

Noticed he was chatting with another guy.

Deke's colleague compared both faces to those on record in the D.C., Maryland and Virginia departments of motor vehicles databases. Got hits on both men within minutes.

Turner Kinney of McLean, Virginia. A private investigator and faux trash hauler.

Earnest Deveraux of Georgetown. Address on the street just ahead where the truck had turned. Mr. Deveraux's occupation was listed as a political consultant.

"Deveraux spells his first name with an 'a' " Deke told Leo. "Like that's supposed to make him more trustworthy."

Leo just grinned and shook his head.

McGill's two henchmen cruised by the street where the truck had turned.

Having glimpsed a Metro PD patrol unit on the scene.

With its lights flashing.

Inigo de Loyola lay curled up on the landing of the front stoop of the Georgetown townhouse, the delightful leather sack filled with cash under his head once more. The concrete surface was no match for the comfortable hospital bed from which he'd been summoned, but it was a familiar sort of resting place nonetheless. One that had allowed the Jesuit easily to succumb to the demands of his tired body.

It seemed he'd been asleep for less time than the Church needed to condemn a heretic — him, for instance — when he felt a hand on his shoulder, shaking him none too gently.

"Come on, old timer," a gruff voice told him, "time to wake up and move on."

De Loyola saw two uniformed policemen, one black, one white.

"Time for breakfast already?" the priest asked.

The two cops looked at each other. They'd responded to a call. An anonymous neighbor had called the department to report a vagrant sleeping on private property. Couldn't have that become a trend. It'd kill real estate values. Spread crime.

Officers Timpkins and Fabach had found and approached the sleeping figure with caution. You never knew what street people might find in their travels: hammers, knives, even firearms if they got into burglary. Their state-of-mind upon wakening would be another unknown consideration. Caution was their watchword.

Both cops had hands on the butts of their duty weapons. But neither was a hardass. A guy who had to sleep outdoors but could wake up cracking a joke, he deserved a little slack.

"You hungry, Pops?" Timpkins asked.

De Loyola pushed himself into a sitting position.

"Not quite so much as most times," he said. "I ate last night, and I have some sandwiches I might share with you, if you need food."

Timpkins and Fabach smiled. Neither had ever had a street person offer them food before.

Officer Timpkins smiled and asked, "What you got?"

"Roast beef, ham and chicken."

"Where'd you get all that?" Fabach wanted to know.

"A kind man took pity on me last night."

"You talk pretty smooth, Pops. You have yourself some education?"

"Several years in the seminary," de Loyola said.

Both cops saw a light go on upstairs in the townhouse. The homeowner had finally noticed the little drama playing out on his doorstep. The cops would have to adopt a sterner demeanor when he appeared. Show him his tax money wasn't being misspent.

Until then, Fabach asked politely, "Are you a priest?"

De Loyola nodded, accepted a hand from Timpkins as he got to his feet.

"I am a Jesuit, yes," de Loyola said.

"Well, what are you doing out here, Father?" Fabach had never heard of a homeless priest.

"Ministering to those who need me."

"People in Georgetown?" Timpkins asked.

"Those who exist on the leavings of the rich," de Loyola said.

"What's in the bag, Father?" Fabach asked.

A light went on just inside the front door and they all heard footsteps descending a staircase.

De Loyola said, "I don't know. I was walking by, saw the bag and thought it might make a fine pillow. It did. But I didn't open it."

"So it's not yours?" Timpkins said, reaching for the bag.

"No," de Loyola told him.

Officer Timpkins unzipped the bag just as the front door opened.

A man wearing pajamas and a navy blue robe looked out at the two cops and the scruffy priest on his stoop and demanded, "What the hell is —"

He stopped talking when he saw the bagful of cash the black cop was holding.

The sick expression of guilt on his face reminded Timpkins of the only other time he ever saw anyone look like that. The night he'd caught his first wife in bed with the guy who lived in the apartment across the hall. Timpkins had been tempted to coldcock this sucker, too.

Now, he asked, "What's your name, sir?"

"Earnest Deveraux."

Timpkins saw a slip of white paper among the jumble of loose greenbacks. He plucked it out and read the message inscribed on it aloud: "'Deveraux. Payment in full.' Looks like this is yours, sir."

Earnest Deveraux took a step back as Timpkins extended the bag to him.

Before the exchange could be made, the roar of a large engine filled the air and a trash-hauling truck came racing down the block. The driver saw the flashing lights of the patrol car parked in the middle of the street and hit his brakes. The tires locked and the huge vehicle skidded forward.

The four men on the stoop looked on in horror.

"My patrol car," Timpkins moaned.

The truck climbed the trunk of the patrol unit and crushed the roof, pushing the cop car another thirty feet along the street. The driver, dazed, popped the door open. He shook his head once, saw the cops, Deveraux and de Loyola staring at him.

Lights were coming on in homes up and down the street now.

Timpkins, the senior officer, yelled, "Fabach, go cuff that sonofabitch who killed my car."

The driver leaped into the street and took off running. He didn't stand a chance. Officer Lorenz Fabach was the 400-meter gold medalist at the Mid-Atlantic Police Olympics. He caught the truck driver before he got twenty meters.

A car bearing a thin woman and a videographer arrived in time to get footage of Fabach bringing his prisoner back to Deveraux's stoop. Both Deveraux and the truck driver avoided looking at each other or the videocam. The homeowner declared he had no knowledge of the money and refused to take possession of it.

Officer Timpkins called for detectives.

The detectives called Captain Rockelle Bullard.

Like Father de Loyola, she pretended she didn't know anything about the money.

The president had left her bed. She and her chief of staff were waiting in the White House library when McGill arrived. He greeted them with a smile. Patti got a hug, too.

"All's well?" the president asked.

McGill nodded. He sat on a love-seat, the open cushion beckoning to Patti.

Galia remained on her feet.

"What's the latest?" the chief of staff asked.

McGill said, "We should probably turn on the TV in a few minutes. Ellie Booker has video of a private detective named Turner Kinney being arrested after he crashed a stolen trash-hauling truck into and atop of a Metro PD patrol car. Kinney has been identified as taking a White House tour with a man named Earnest, with an 'a,' Deveraux."

Galia sat down and entered the names into her laptop computer.

Patti asked McGill, "Deveraux was the man who planted the money behind your office?"

He said, "The garbage truck versus cop car crash happened directly opposite Deveraux's townhouse. I also got his name from Ellie Booker. He was working with SNAM, Satellite News America."

The president compressed her lips. "God, I despise those tabloid cretins."

"Yeah," McGill said, "that first amendment can be damn inconvenient. Anyway, Ms. Booker kindly told me that a SNAM reporter, a fellow who drives a red Mini Cooper, recently made a visit to a local emergency room with facial bruises, lacerations and even one good bite mark. Said he'd gotten into a pub brawl and the docs and nurses should see the other guy."

"He was the one who got into the fight with the priest?"

"Yeah, and Father de Loyola gave better than he got. What I figure is, the reporter knew all about the money behind my office. Figured maybe he should grab some for himself, before he splashed the news on SNAM. Who would ever call him on it?"

"No one, if Father de Loyola hadn't been there."

McGill smiled. "Elspeth told me she talked to the good father earlier last night. He was standing on Pennsylvania Avenue, facing the White House and praying. He told Elspeth he was praying for you and everyone who lived and worked here."

Patti's eyes moistened. She kissed McGill. "Thank you for telling me that."

Galia cleared her throat. The First Couple took notice of her.

"Earnest Deveraux is a new arrival in town. He previously worked as a lobbyist in Baton Rouge, Louisiana. People in the legislature there say he always gets his way in the end. Whether it's a matter of spreading big money around or playing dirty tricks, it's all the same to him. He came to Washington in February. Perhaps the most significant thing about him is that his cousin was the late Bobby Beckley."

Beckley had been the chief of staff and top fund raiser for the late, murdered-in-his-own-home Senator Howard Hurlbert, the president's longtime political nemesis and the second-place finisher in the last presidential election. Politics had been a blood sport for

Beckley. Aptly, he'd been found floating in his swimming pool, the victim of a snake bite.

McGill sighed.

The president looked at him and said, "What?"

"I also got a call from Dikki Missirian. I was glad to hear from him because I needed a favor. But he and Max Lucey saw a Cadillac limo pull out behind the stolen trash-hauling truck and the red Mini Cooper that hightailed it away from my office building this morning. Dikki videoed the limo with his cell-phone.

"He e-mailed the video clip to me and Elspeth ran the plate for me."

Patti and Galia both said, "Whose car is it?"

McGill said, "Originally, it was Howard Hurlbert's. Title is now held by his widow, Bettina."

Father Inigo de Loyola was standing on Pennsylvania Avenue outside the White House praying again that morning. The sky was cloudless and the sun warm. A soft breeze from the west kept the humidity low. A tired Elspeth Kendry waited for the Jesuit's eyes to open before she spoke to him.

"Beautiful morning, Father. Nice to see you again."

"A joy to speak with you also, my child," he replied. "Have I overstayed my welcome?"

The special agent in charge of the White House Security Detail shook her head.

"Stop by anytime. You do good work."

"I try my best."

"I would feel better if I knew you had a roof over your head," Elspeth said.

The Jesuit beamed.

"Oh, but I have. Mr. McGill found a place for me."

"He did?"

"Yes. A friend of his owns some properties."

"Dikki Missirian?"

"The very person. A kind and gentle man. He showed me his office on P Street. He offered me space beneath a staircase in another building. It's just the place for someone like me."

Lost Dog

McGill Short Case #2

M cGill never had a kid for a client before. He'd seen plenty of kids in trouble, including little ones, during his days as a Chicago Police Department patrol officer. He'd dealt with wayward affluent teenagers and college students when he was the chief of police in Winnetka, Illinois. Since going into the private investigations business in Washington, DC, though, he'd only worked cases brought to him by adults.

Until today when a forlorn dark-haired sprite in a deep blue jacket and skirt with vaguely naval tailoring took a seat in front of his desk.

She couldn't be more than eight years old, McGill thought, if he remembered his own daughters' growth patterns right. She was just about to speak when McGill held up a finger, stopping her. He smiled when he did it so she wouldn't think he was a grumpy old guy.

"One minute, sweetheart. I'll be right back."

The kid took the interruption in stride. Sat with her hands folded on her lap. Her feet were a good six inches off the floor. Maybe she was only seven years old, McGill thought.

He poked his head into the outer office. Sweetie was behind her desk, having a staring contest with a guy McGill first thought might be a European relative of Celsus Crogher. He was that white. On second look, though, this character's pallor had a metallic tinge to it, as if he buffed himself up with silverware polish.

"Margaret?" McGill said.

"Yes?"

Sweetie kept her unblinking eyes on the guy; he didn't bother looking at McGill either.

"The young girl in my office, she's with this gentleman?"

"She came in with him, asked for you. Her name is Anya, she said. This guy didn't introduce himself. Just sat down. Gave me the stink eye. He's been working it ever since."

"Good luck with that, pal," McGill told the man. Sweetie could make the devil blink first, McGill knew. At least any devil he'd ever seen her interrogate. "I'll leave the door open."

Sweetie gave McGill a slight wave of acknowledgment.

Never breaking eye contact with the creepy guy.

McGill went back into his office to talk with the kid. He took a seat in his second guest chair instead of sitting behind his desk. He was closer to the kid that way. Offering more of a paternal feeling than a professional one, he hoped.

The kid called him on it.

"Why are you sitting there instead of there?" She pointed to McGill's empty chair behind the desk. The kid had an accent. A combination of accents, really. A British intonation overlaying something that sounded Eastern European to his ear.

He shrugged. "This is my office. I can sit where I like."

Young as she was, the girl understood the assertion of authority.

"Of course," she said.

McGill also didn't want anything between him and the outer office if the competition between Sweetie and the guy out there turned physical.

He asked the kid, "Did you come here with the man waiting outside my office?"

She nodded. "His name is Georgi. He is my driver."

"Does Georgi do anything else for you?"

Her face said he did, but she was reluctant to give it up.

"Maybe Georgi helps keep you safe," McGill suggested.

"Yes, he does that, too."

"Does Georgi carry a gun?"

The girl pressed her lips firmly together.

"I'll take that as a yes," McGill said.

He raised his voice and passed the information on to Sweetie.

Got a perfunctory "Uh-huh" in reply. Sweetie was still locked in visual combat.

"So your name is Anya?" McGill asked the kid.

"Anya Ivanova."

"What can I do for you, Anya?" McGill asked.

"My dog ran away. I would like you to find him."

She reached into a pocket of her jacket. Brought out a picture and handed it to McGill. Her chin started to quiver. Her eyes grew moist. McGill handed her a tissue from the box on his desk; more than one client had needed them. He looked at the photo.

The beast was black, smallish and had a pugnacious air to it despite having a face that seemed to be more fur than clearly defined features. McGill had never seen the breed before.

Anya said, "His name is Misha. He is an Affenpinscher."

"Friendly?" McGill asked.

Wouldn't do to find the kid's dog only to have to shoot it if it attacked.

"You must win his friendship. Then he will be your best friend."

Spoken like a kid who didn't have any other friends, McGill felt.

He wasn't busy at the moment. Thought it wouldn't hurt to put in a few hours and see if he could help out. Throw a net over the mutt, if it came to that. Anya, more likely than not, was a diplomat's kid. Maybe he could do a good deed and help foreign relations.

"Is Georgi your father, Anya?"

The girl rolled her eyes.

"No?" McGill said. "You know I charge for my services, don't you?"

He might have put in a few hours for free if Georgi hadn't

given Sweetie the stink eye.

"Yes, of course, I know." She reached into her pocket again and brought out a check for McGill. "I hope this will be enough money."

McGill looked at the check.

Three days pay. Calculated to the penny.

The money was drawn on an account of the embassy of the Russian Federation.

McGill proposed a deal to the kid. She'd keep her check. He'd look for the dog for up to but no more than three days. If he found Misha, they'd work out a payment for no more than the amount of the check. If he didn't find her pet, he would express his regrets and eat his expenses.

"Eat?" Anya asked, not understanding.

"I won't charge you for my time."

"But you are in business, yes?"

"I am."

"How can this be good for you, not to take money for your work?"

"Well, I can't do this with everyone, but sometimes it's smart to buy good will."

The kid gave him another look of puzzlement.

McGill explained, "Let's say I don't find Misha. You'll feel bad; I'll feel bad. But you'll know, because I didn't take your money, that I was really trying to help you. Then maybe when you're older and you need some help, you'll come back to me."

"Why would I, if you can't find Misha?"

McGill repressed a grin. The kid was sharp. He liked her.

From the outer office came the sound of Sweetie laughing.

Followed by the door to the stairwell opening and closing.

"What is funny?" Anya asked. "Did your lady friend just leave?"

Sweetie appeared in the doorway to McGill's office.

The kid looked at her and blinked. "Did Georgi leave?"

Her voice held a note of disbelief.

Sweetie said, "He stepped outside for a moment."

McGill asked Anya, "Would you like us to take you to him?"

She said, "I would like you to find Misha."

"Okay," McGill said, "if we can do it my way. To answer your question: If I can't find Misha, you wouldn't come back to me if you'd lost another dog. But if you had another kind of problem, one you thought I could help with, then you might come back to me. That's what I meant by good will."

"Because I would know you want to help me, not just take my money," Anya said.

"Exactly," McGill told her.

Anya told him where she always walked her dog.

During daylight hours, that was. Household staff gave Misha his evening walk.

The dog got away from one Yuri Melnikov the previous evening.

She said those were the only clues she could offer.

McGill asked, "Does Misha have a favorite treat?"

Anya gave McGill a nod. Not just as a preliminary answer to his question. She was glad to see he was already thinking of ways to solve her problem.

"He favors bits of braised beef," she said.

Pricy, McGill thought. That led him to ask, "Anya, what does your mother or father do here in Washington?"

"My mother," the girl said, "is the senior counselor for cultural affairs at our embassy."

Anya dug into her pocket again and gave McGill her mother's business card.

"Where do you go to school?"

"I am tutored at home."

As if to forestall any more questions, Anya got to her feet and stuck out her hand.

McGill shook it.

***

Sweetie explained her victory to McGill as the simple triumph of good over evil.

"You think Georgi's a bad guy?"

"Yeah, he is. I looked into his eyes long enough to see that."

"How bad?" McGill asked.

"Blood-on-his-hands bad. Maybe even body-count bad."

"A guy like that is babysitting a young girl?" McGill asked.

"Maybe the kid's parents have enemies. We'd all do anything to protect our kids, right?"

Sweetie had only recently become a *de facto* stepmother to her husband's orphaned niece, Maxine. The plan was she and Putnam would adopt the girl as soon as Maxi was willing to accept that Mom and Dad wouldn't be coming back. Already, though, Sweetie was willing to die — or if given no other choice, kill — for her.

Just as McGill would do for any of his three children.

"Helluva thing," he said.

Sweetie told him, "I could be overdramatizing."

McGill's phone rang. FBI Deputy Director Byron DeWitt was on the line.

"Do you know who you just had in your office?" he asked.

"Anya Ivanova."

"Yes, and Georgi Travkin of the Russian Federal Security Service."

McGill asked, "Do you spell that K-G-B?"

"You might, if you were feeling nostalgic. He has a diplomatic cover, of course."

"So you weren't snooping on me?" McGill said. "You were keeping an eye on Georgi."

"Right." DeWitt paused. "The Bureau has been warned not overstep with you."

Especially after Special Agent Osgood Riddick came to grief, McGill thought.

He asked, "Who passed the word, SAC Kendry or Galia Mindel?"

"The president."

McGill felt all warm inside; his wife was looking out for him.

In the glow of the moment, he asked DeWitt, "Would you like to know why Anya came to see me?"

"Very much, if you don't mind sharing."

"Young Ms. Ivanova would like me to find her missing dog, Misha."

DeWitt took McGill at his word. Warned him Georgi Travkin was dangerous.

McGill hung up and told Sweetie, "You know who you just stared down?"

She didn't, so he told her.

"Hope he doesn't take it the wrong way," Sweetie said.

McGill replied, "He might resent being laughed at."

McGill stopped outside the Oval Office and asked the president's personal secretary, Edwina Byington, "How goes the ship of state?"

"The seamanship is superb," she told him. "The weather could be better."

"Not a good time to drop in?"

"Let me check. Sometimes you're just the dose of Dramamine the president needs."

McGill smiled. He hoped Edwina put that line in her memoirs. She buzzed the president and got a quick reply.

"Five minutes, Mr. McGill."

"Thank you, Edwina." The woman was a treasure. He thought she might even be able to help him with his problem of the moment. "Edwina, do you know anyone who knows dogs?"

She nodded and gestured McGill to her guest chair.

"That would be me, to a lesser degree, and my son and my granddaughter to a greater degree. Marshal is a veterinarian and Camilla breeds Vizslas."

Happy days, McGill thought. Expert help close at hand.

"Have you ever heard of an Affenpinscher?" he asked.

"Yes. They're small dogs, said to have a monkey-like face,

though I never saw that. They're very loyal to their owners, but can be territorial and even aggressive with strangers or other animals. They won't back down from a fight. I've also heard they're hard to housebreak."

"What about running away from home? Are they known to do that?"

"Not that I've heard. That wouldn't fit with being owner loyal, would it?"

"No," McGill said, "it wouldn't. And if they're aggressive with strangers, it probably wouldn't be a good idea to grab one bare-handed."

Edwina shook her head. "Even a small dog can have a big bite."

McGill carried those words of wisdom with him into the Oval Office.

Galia Mindel, the White House chief of staff, had been in with the president before McGill arrived. She was about to leave as McGill entered. He asked Galia if she might stay for a few minutes. Galia looked to the president for approval and got a nod.

The president remained in place behind her desk and McGill and Galia sat opposite her.

"What can we do for you, Jim?" the president asked.

McGill told her, "The Russians want to hire me."

"What?" Galia asked.

McGill gave the chief of staff a glance, then told the president, "I thought I should run the idea by you first, but the truth is the kid and I shook on it."

Galia was about to ask what kid, but the president forestalled her with a gesture.

McGill used the opening to explain the situation.

"Have you ever found a dog before, Jim?" the president asked.

He shook his head. "Never lost one, never had one."

The president said, "Neither did I. My mother was allergic."

"Mine, too."

The two of them grinned and shook their heads.

There was always something new to learn about your spouse.

Galia said, "Isn't this something Ms. Sweeney could handle?"

McGill told them about Sweetie staring down the KGB guy.

"I'd like to have seen that," the president said.

"As would I," Galia admitted.

"Anyway," McGill said, "the kid came to me."

"But there's no written agreement and you didn't accept payment," Galia said, asking for confirmation of those points.

McGill nodded.

Galia opined that no political harm had been done so far.

McGill said, "There's a couple of things that bother me."

The president knew what her husband was thinking.

"Sure, you're wondering if the Russians are playing you somehow, and is Anya is on it?"

"Caitie could have done it at that age," McGill said.

He and Patti were having a dinner for two in the private dining room of the Residence, the president's living quarters at the White House.

"I agree," Patti said, "and some parents aren't averse to making use of their children."

The president wore a slightly mocking smile as she delivered her line.

McGill had once involved his younger daughter to help confront the Reverend Burke Godfrey in front of hundreds of his agitated followers. Of course, Caitie was in the close company of Margaret Sweeney. The Secret Service and Metro cops were close by, too. Even so, there was no telling what might have happened.

McGill shook his head and sighed.

"I still have the occasional nightmare about how that could have gone wrong, and exposing Caitie to a mob certainly ticked off Carolyn." McGill's ex, Caitie's mother.

"Scared me, too," Patti said, "though you're the only one to whom I can admit that. But everything worked out well, and Caitie got the national exposure that led to her acting career."

"I'm not too sure I'd put that in my ledger's asset column. Might turn out to be a smack to my backside in the long run."

The president shook her head. "I have my people in Los Angeles looking out for her."

"You mean your show biz people?"

Patti Grant had been in the movies before entering politics.

"Yes."

"Spying on Caitie?"

"Yes."

McGill nodded. "I approve entirely."

"I wanted to give you plausible deniability, but now that's out the window."

"No problem. But talking things through just now, I can see how the moment of tears and anxiety Anya showed in my office could have been a performance. She said she has tutors. Maybe one of them is a drama coach."

"Could well be, considering Irina Ivanova worked in Russian films."

"An actress?" McGill asked.

Patti nodded.

"And you found that out in the past two hours?" McGill asked.

"Galia can work wonders. She also found Irina's most recent movie for us to see; subtitles are being added to the film right now."

"Can we have popcorn while we watch?" McGill asked.

"The Russians serve caviar at the movies."

McGill wrinkled his nose.

Patti said, "I've heard the Norwegians like to eat dried reindeer meat at the cinema."

That made McGill laugh. "Yeah, give me a jumbo serving of that."

"Very well, popcorn it is," Patti said, "but, Jim, I'd like you to keep two things in mind."

"Little Anya didn't find my name in the Yellow Pages?"

"That's one."

"Misha the Missing Mutt might serve a purpose other than keeping the kid company?"

"Very good. Full marks," Patti said.

The two of them finished dinner.

Then McGill headed out to Montrose Park before it got dark.

He took Deke Ky and Leo Levy with him.

He brought a plastic bag filled with bits of braised beef, too.

Leftovers from dinner.

The Russian Embassy was on Wisconsin Avenue. Montrose Park was just east of that thoroughfare and immediately south of Dumbarton Oaks Park and the U.S. Naval Observatory, the grounds of which were home to the vice president's official residence. On the southern fringe of Montrose Park lay Rock Creek. Following that watercourse to the Northeast would bring you to the National Zoological Park.

Besides the nearby zoo, Montrose Park offered such amenities as tennis courts, playgrounds, picnic tables and an exercise course. In some places, it was a perfectly civilized green-space for tony Georgetown. In other spots, it was a woodland wilderness that left behind the sights and sounds of the modern world.

Any conscientious urban mother would keep a close eye on her offspring in the built-up areas, and unless mom had Outward Bound experience, she'd probably keep her kids out of the woods altogether. Two-legged predators were more than enough to worry about.

Then again, a small fry with an armed, experienced and possibly deadly escort, e.g. the melanin-depleted Georgi Travkin, might feel a bit more daring.

McGill felt safe in the mid-May twilight with his Secret Service bodyguard, Deke Ky; Leo stayed with the car. For that matter, McGill was also armed. None of the other visitors to the park seemed to be carrying a weapon. Of course, you never knew what someone might stash in a fanny-pack.

What was perfectly obvious, people in Montrose Park liked to unleash their hounds.

McGill asked Deke, "How many free-range dogs do you see out there?"

He was sure Deke would know, in case one of the pups showed hostile intent.

"Nine," Deke said.

"You see any Affenpinschers?"

"Is that a trick question?"

"You're not a dog guy?"

Deke said, "On my mom's side of the family, they eat dogs."

"I thought that was a tall tale."

"Unh-uh. In Vietnam, eating dog is said to bring good fortune."

"What kind of good fortune?"

"The kind that says you won't starve that day."

McGill gave Deke a look. They'd been together over four years now. In the absence of either Deke's superiors or the media, their relationship was informal. In the second term of the Grant administration, apparently, it was going to be jocular, too.

With a gleam in his Afro-Eurasian blue eyes, Deke added, "Dog meat is also supposed to be good for stoking the male libido."

McGill grinned. "What with so many guys being hounds at heart."

Deke liked that and nodded.

He said, "I see a Chocolate Lab, a Golden Retriever, a Beagle, a German Shepherd mix and five I-don't-know-whats."

"So you know more than you let on," McGill said, "but what kind of libation do you serve with a dog entrée?"

"Yellow Snow IPA."

McGill laughed. "If that's a real brand, dinner at Morton's is on me."

"I'll give you a copy of the tab."

McGill and Deke observed the folkways of the dog owners for

a few minutes. The people conversed as happily as their beasties cavorted. Peaceful kingdom. Everyone picked up his or her animal's droppings. Tied off the biodegradable bags and tossed them into a dedicated receptacle.

Talk about a nasty job, emptying that thing.

"Alpha dog and owner?" McGill asked.

"Shepherd mix with the guy attracting all the ladies."

"My thought, too. Let's go over and have a chat."

Having no canine companion to call their own, McGill and Deke drew several curious looks from the dog lovers they approached. Then one young woman recognized McGill and smiled. She looked as if she might say something to him, got a look from Deke — serious as a tumor — and decided to keep her thought to herself.

"It's okay," McGill told her, "my friend bites only when I tell him to."

"You're the president's husband, aren't you?" she asked.

The other women with her leaned forward to get a better look.

The guy who owned the Shepherd stayed cool, quiet and right where he was.

"Much to my good fortune, I am," McGill said.

"Where's your dog?" another woman asked.

"I don't have one."

"You never got one for your kids?" the first woman asked.

"Their mother is allergic."

Just like his mother, McGill thought. He'd never thought of that before.

"That's a shame."

The Shepherd owner spoke up. "Is there something we might do to help you?"

McGill looked at the guy. Smiled. Understood the situation. The Shepherd guy didn't care to share his spotlight but was being polite about it. Fair enough.

"I'm looking for a lost dog for a client," he said to the guy. Turning to the women, he added, "It's an Affenpinscher." He showed them the picture Anya had given him.

Several of the women said they'd seen the animal; none of them knew its name.

"Misha," the Shepherd guy provided. "Little girl named Anya walks him when the sun's up. Russian guy name of Yuri handles dusk patrol."

The lady dog owners were impressed. So was McGill.

"Are you a cop?" he asked.

"Used to be. Then I got my business degree. Now, I do investigations for insurance companies." He extended his hand to McGill. "Steve Nagy."

McGill shook his hand. "Jim McGill."

He added, "What else can you tell me about Misha and Yuri?"

"Misha has a misplaced sense of badass. He charged Ajax one time."

Nagy whistled and his Shepherd mix, which had been busy running circles around two other dogs, sprinted to the insurance investigator's side, sat and looked at the nearby humans. The dog ladies were old friends. McGill passed muster, too. When Ajax cast his eyes on Deke, though, his ruff went up and a low growl started at the back of his throat.

Nagy gave the beast a pat on a shoulder and he went bounding back to play.

With one look back at Deke, to make sure he didn't try anything funny.

"Ajax is a good dog. He could've snapped Misha's head off, but he just stuck his snout under the runt's middle and flipped him twenty feet or so through the air."

"Misha learned the error of his ways?" McGill asked.

"Oh, yeah."

"What about Yuri? Did he have anything to say?"

"He looked pissed, but Ajax was sitting at my side, like he was just now, and I don't think Yuri liked his chances. He gave me his business card, very carefully, and told me I'd be hearing from his embassy."

"Did you?" McGill asked.

"Anya introduced herself to me the next day. She brought me two box seat tickets to a Nationals game with the Dodgers next week. Asked me to accept her apology for Misha's misbehavior. Said she didn't let her dog off the leash. Then, bold as brass, she offered Ajax a sniff at the back of her hand. He slurped it and all was well."

"Almost," McGill said. "Misha got away from Yuri again and hasn't come home."

"Oh, I saw that," the woman who'd recognized McGill said. "The dog running away, I mean. He was off the leash again, and this time he ran into the woods. I didn't think anything of it. Thought he'd come back when he got tired or hungry. I've seen him come out of the trees before."

The insurance investigator's business degree kicked in.

"Is there a reward for finding Misha?" he asked.

McGill was about to say a hundred bucks.

Then he remembered he was in Georgetown.

"Five hundred dollars. For the genuine article. In one piece and mint condition."

The Shepherd owner looked at Deke.

"Would you have shot Ajax if he made a move on you?"

"You bet."

The dog ladies looked horrified.

McGill told everyone, "You can't mess with the Secret Service."

To help calm nerves, he offered the bits of braised beef to their dogs.

Every dog in the park soon gathered to be fed, and would have liked a second helping.

McGill stared at the screen of the iPad his children had given him for his birthday earlier that month. He and his ex-wife, Carolyn, had given Abbie, Kenny and Caitie the Apple tablets and they'd pooled their money, with an assist from Mom, to return the favor.

The McGills used the devices to Skype with one another — after federal government tech wizards had modified them for secure communications.

Carolyn's birthday was in June; that was when she'd get her specialized iPad.

Patti already had one.

At the moment, McGill, sitting in his hideaway at the White House, was using his tablet to pore over a road map of Northwest Washington, DC. Patti entered the room, sat next to her husband and handed him a glass of ice tea. She had one of her own. McGill gave her a smile of thanks and went back to studying the map.

"I thought you knew your way around town pretty well by now," Patti said.

"I do, generally. Leo has gotten to know the metro area like a cabbie. His GPS can find the places new to both of us. Right now, I'm trying to look at things from a canine point of view."

"Putting your nose to the ground, so to speak," Patti said.

McGill smiled at Patti, giving her his full attention now.

"You know how far a dog can travel to find its way home?"

Patti shook her head. "No idea."

"From what I've read so far, at least five hundred miles."

"Dogs are good with maps?"

"No," McGill said, "they're great with a sense of smell."

Patti said, "They can smell home from five hundred miles? You're kidding."

"No. That's a surmise, but one informed by a veterinary degree."

"I bow to the experts," Patti said. "But what's a dog's motivation to walk so far, love?"

"Love, loyalty, maybe the opportunity to chew the shoes of whoever turned him out."

Patti asked, "Are you thinking of your young client? Not that she turned her dog out, but returning to her would be going home, wouldn't it?"

"It would, if the dog was able to get home."

Patti thought about that for a moment, before asking, "You have an idea why the dog *wouldn't* be able to sniff its way home?"

McGill told Patti of little Misha's encounter with great big Ajax.

"That made me wonder if maybe the tough little mutt tried to fight outside its weight class with another big canine. Say some beast unrestrained by domestication and a watchful master. My thinking was maybe it ran into a coyote."

"In Washington, the city proper?"

McGill nodded at his font of electronic wisdom. "A coyote was first observed in Rock Creek Park in 2004. Sightings have been reported regularly since then."

The president *hmmed*. "I seem to remember reading of coyotes in California attacking young children. We can't have that."

McGill never ceased to be amazed by a president's range of concerns.

"Wouldn't be good," he agreed. He had something else to add but held back.

Patti saw McGill's self-restraint and asked, "Is there something you'd like to know?"

He told her, "I've tried to stay out of politics as much as I could, but I seem to keep getting drawn into things lately. I don't know if I should try harder to steer clear or just yield to the inevitable."

"Let your president be your guide," Patti said.

"Okay. Is there anything I should know regarding what you and Galia were talking about when I barged in on you?"

Patti thought about it. "There's no harm in your knowing. You're not a blabbermouth."

"Certainly not."

"True South is looking to rebrand itself. Politically, they'll remain hard right, but they want a label that's more national than regional. Some Democrats in certain states who rely on right-of-center voters to hold their seats might switch parties if True South finds an appealing new name."

"Complicating your life even more," McGill said.

"Galia isn't taking things lying down. There are others in

Congress who are currently in the GOP and depend on moderate voters to stay in office. We might be roping in some of them."

McGill blinked. "Is the Republican Party about to go defunct?"

"Maybe the Democratic Party, too. Or it could become a coalition partner with a new progressive party on the left."

"Wow. How's all this change going to work out?"

"Nobody knows, but it might be for the best. The two old major parties look like they've come to the end of their useful lives. Political evolution could be good for everybody."

McGill grinned. "Yeah, except for those people who don't believe in evolution."

"I didn't say it would be easy," Patti said. Changing the subject, she asked, "What else have you found out about dogs?"

McGill tapped his iPad screen.

A photo of a World War One soldier appeared. Next to the doughboy was a dog. Both of them looked scuffed up but ready for action.

McGill told Patti, "In the so-called Great War, when frontline commanders needed to get a message back to headquarters, the most successful means of communications often was to use dogs as messengers."

"Interesting but how is that relevant to your case?" Patti asked.

McGill said, "Dogs are analog technology not digital. You can't wiretap a dog. If the animal is smart and fast, you'd be hard pressed even to throw a net over him. I won't ask you if the NSA or some other spook shop has tapped into every diplomatic mission in town. But if that's the case, maybe the people at the Russian embassy decided to go old school."

"You think Anya's dog was a courier? Communicating with whom? For what purpose?"

"That's what I hope to find out tomorrow," McGill replied.

McGill coaxed Leo out of the new whiz-bang Chevy sedan the government provided to keep McGill safe and mobile. Members of

Congress from both the GOP and True South recently had offered public opinions that since McGill used the car for his private business he should reimburse the Treasury for the privilege. McGill said fine by him.

Adding, "So long as the same requirement applies to any future presidential spouse who continues to work after moving into the White House."

Neither party on the right anticipated electing a female president any time soon. Enough social progress had been made in their ranks, though, to anticipate that their next First Lady might insist on keeping her day job after her husband became president. Jabbing McGill was all in good fun; sticking one of their own with the cost of leasing an exotically equipped car was another matter.

The issue was referred to committee for further consideration and discussion.

Meaning McGill would probably get a free ride for another four years.

Leo was agreeable to leaving his beloved ride because McGill had told him that he and Deke needed someone with tracking and hunting experience to help them. Leo took a shotgun out of the new arsenal in the Chevy's trunk. Locked the car tight. Armed its anti-theft measures. Felt certain it would remain right where he left it, undisturbed. The car could be vandalized, of course, but it would make a video of the perpetrator. Send Leo a distress signal, too.

As the three men approached the woods adjacent to Montrose Park shortly after dawn, they saw one other person in the park, Steve Nagy, the insurance investigator. He was throwing a ragged yellow tennis ball high into the air. Paying keen attention and getting a jump on the ball's trajectory that any major league outfielder would admire, Ajax raced off to make the catch.

The dog snatched the ball out of the air cleanly and ran it back to Nagy.

Ajax stopped to look at the three newcomers. McGill waved and said hello to Nagy. Ajax watched Deke, but didn't demonstrate any audible aggression. He'd obviously been taught a lesson by Nagy and took it to heart.

McGill admired the dog's qualities. Wondered how Patti might feel about getting one.

Nagy waved and smiled.

Didn't bat an eye at Leo carrying the shotgun at his shoulder.

"Handsome animal," Leo said as they stepped into the woods.

Deke agreed, "Yeah, it'd look real good turning on a spit over an open fire."

Leo gave his friend a strange look. Turned his attention to McGill.

"Okay, boss, the way I heard you, we're looking for any signs of a coyote and/or the remains of a small dog."

Checking the photo Anya gave him, McGill said, "Yeah, the dog wore a red collar with a metal tag. Maybe a rabies inoculation record or something."

"Gotcha," Leo said, "and how far do you want me to track?"

"Let's take it to the far side of the zoo."

"Then we turn around?" Deke asked.

"No, then we step out into the manicured part of Rock Creek Park and see if we can spot someone — man, woman or child — looking for little Misha on that end."

The three of them set off, only the good ol' boy having any idea of what he was doing.

McGill noticed that Leo's fieldcraft had a distinctly casual air to it. He didn't beat any bushes; he nudged them aside with a shoe. Moved on without comment when his effort failed to turn up any remnant of cleanly gnawed canine carcass. There were piles of animal poop along the way, though one or two made McGill think that members of his own kind were among those who shat in the woods.

Leo simply stepped over the deposits of feces and said, "Nope, that ain't what we're lookin' for."

Deke, as was his role, kept an eye out to make sure no male-factor popped out from behind a tree with a weapon and hostile intent. Taking the rear guard position, he also made sure nobody sneaked up on them from behind. Like McGill, though, he would have been more at home in an urban setting.

Leo set a steady pace and before long they exited the trees into a more refined stretch of Rock Creek Park. McGill and Deke felt more comfortable immediately. But Leo said, "That was fun. I haven't been out for a hike like that in too long a time."

"We didn't find anything," Deke said.

McGill told him, "We narrowed things down."

"How's that?" Deke asked.

"It looks like Misha didn't get eaten anywhere near where he was last seen. Is that a fair assumption, Leo?"

The driver nodded.

"If he'd been taken by a single coyote, one who thought he'd better finish his meal quick before some other critter came along and wanted to share, I'd have seen the spot where the coyote settled down for his meal. We'd probably have found the dog's skull, too. If the coyote had been the alpha member of a family group, we'd have seen several sets of tracks, smelled their pee and some poop."

"Didn't know you were such a Dan'l Boone," Deke told Leo.

"Sure," Leo told him, "when I was a boy, I went out into the woods with my trusty .22 single shot every weekend. Right after Hebrew School."

McGill smiled. Deke rolled his eyes.

"We learn anything else?" the special agent asked.

Looking into the distance, McGill saw something and nodded. "Come on," he said.

He led the other two to a light pole on which a sheet of paper had been taped. On the flyer was a photograph of a small dog. This time, McGill did see a certain resemblance between the dog's face and that of a monkey. The animal in the picture was wearing a collar with a tag.

The message above the photo said: *Lost Dog.*

Deke pointed out the obvious. "That says the dog's name is ZuZu."

"Uh-huh," McGill agreed. "Look up the contact phone number listed there. See who it belongs to."

There were no unlisted numbers in the database the feds used, if it was a landline.

Deke found the number's subscriber and told McGill in a flat voice: "Embassy of the People's Republic of China."

Leo whistled. "Russians, Chinese, this pooch is a real commie."

"Maybe," McGill said. "What's interesting is, I was told Affenpinschers are loyal to specific people and hostile to everyone else. Can you think of a better quality for a courier?"

He pulled the Lost Dog notice off the pole. Held it up over his head in both hands. Did a slow three hundred and sixty degree turn.

Deke scanned the horizon and asked, "You think somebody's watching us?"

"Never can tell," McGill said.

Leo took the shotgun off his shoulder. Looked for bad guys. Found none.

McGill said, "We've put in a good morning's work. Let's get back to the office."

He seemed relaxed. Deke and Leo were still on alert.

"One more thing you might think about," Deke said.

"Yeah?" McGill asked.

"The reason the Chinese might've put up that poster? They eat dogs, too."

McGill didn't think FBI Deputy Director Byron DeWitt had been trying to fake him out when he'd called about Georgi Travkin dropping by his office with Anya Ivanova. DeWitt hadn't known anything about Anya's missing dog. That led McGill to the think the Bureau hadn't played a role in Misha's disappearance. Of course, another government agency might be hip deep in the affair.

Sitting behind his desk, McGill called Doctor Daryl Cheveyo at Georgetown University. A secretary answered the call. When McGill identified himself and asked politely if he might speak with the good doctor, he got a positive response.

"Yes, sir. You're on his put-him-through list."

McGill grinned. "Who else is on it?"

"That would be indiscreet, if I were to tell you."

"Which you won't."

"No, sir."

A moment later Cheveyo came on. "Mr. McGill, sir, good to hear from you."

"Thank you, Doctor. I'm hoping you might still be in touch with your former colleagues."

He'd skipped mentioning Cheveyo's erstwhile employer, the CIA, intentionally; you never knew who might be hacking a university phone line.

Cheveyo said, "This isn't something you might pursue through other channels?"

"I'm just looking for a lost dog. I think an informal approach might be best."

"A dog?"

"A small dog — with big friends."

"Okay, then. I might know someone. Are you looking for a personal meeting?"

"Yes, with someone who's a good conversationalist."

Letting Cheveyo know he wanted to meet with someone who wouldn't try to stonewall him.

"You'll hold up your end of the discussion?" Cheveyo asked.

McGill said, "I will."

"I'll get back to you before close of business or a friend will. Where would you like to meet?"

McGill said, "The Nationals just started a home stand. How about we take in a ball game? Hot dogs and popcorn are on me."

Cheveyo didn't seem overwhelmed. Maybe he wasn't a baseball fan.

"You'll leave a ticket at the will-call window?" he asked.

McGill said, "I was thinking more of a skybox. Comfort and privacy. I'm sure the president knows someone who can do a favor."

McGill didn't bother Patti about pulling strings for him.

He brought the matter to Galia Mindel's attention.

The chief of staff said, "Do you know who's pitching tonight?"

McGill didn't. As a Chicago White Sox fan, he didn't pay much attention to the National League. Except to root for whoever was playing the Cubs.

"No, who?"

"Jordan Zimmermann."

McGill had heard of him. He asked, "How's he doing this year?"

"Eight and oh."

Leave it Galia to know baseball stats. She probably followed all the local pro and college teams.

"So you're saying get a sky box to myself will be a problem?" McGill asked.

"To *yourself?*"

"Well, there will be one other person with me."

"It had better be someone important."

"Would you like me to tell you all about it?"

Galia stopped to think. "Not yet, maybe later."

"Sensible answer. So can you do it?"

"Yes, but it's going to cost me."

Better Galia than the president, McGill thought.

Sweetie knocked on McGill's door two minutes after he got off the phone with Galia.

She told him, "Boris is here."

"Who?" McGill asked.

"Okay, it's Georgi, but I've come to think of him as Boris."

"The guy who tried to outstare you?"

"Uh-huh. He didn't want a rematch."

"What would Georgi like?"

"A minute of your time."

"Show him in, Margaret. But stay close. The guy's scary."

Sweetie smiled and gestured to Georgi. He entered McGill's office and stood in front of his desk, declining the offer of a seat.

"Something I can do for you, Mr. Travkin?"

"You know my name?"

"The FBI whispered it to me."

The Russian security man filed that tidbit away in memory.

He told McGill, "Anya would like to know if you've made any progress in finding Misha."

McGill said, "It looks like coyotes haven't eaten him."

The man leaned forward from the waist, as if to aid his comprehension.

"Coyotes?"

"Small wolves."

Now, Georgi leaned back, as if to gauge McGill's honesty.

"You are serious?"

"I am. There are coyotes in Washington, but I'm pretty sure they didn't eat Misha."

"Do you know where the dog is?"

"I can't say for sure, but I think I'm getting closer."

Georgi took a check out of a pocket. The same one Anya had showed him.

He said, "If you are getting closer, will you take payment now?"

"No, thank you. Not quite yet."

"You are sure?"

"I am."

Georgi looked disappointed by McGill, avoided meeting Sweetie's eyes and left.

Sweetie said to McGill, "They probably told him back home it'd be a lot easier to get capitalists to take their money."

McGill replied, "Most other places in Washington, it probably is."

***

Galia Mindel came through for McGill in grand fashion. She got him a Washington Suite, a first level luxury box with a view of the game from almost directly behind home plate. Couldn't ask for better. There was space for at least a couple dozen people, the way McGill saw it.

At the moment, there were only three men present: him, Deke and Leo.

The suite had retractable glass doors, outdoor padded chairs and a private restroom. Food and beverages were provided *en suite* upon request. All three men had been provided with soft drinks. Leo, being a traditionalist, was also enjoying popcorn and a hot dog. The glass doors were closed for the time being.

It was seven o'clock. The game would start in five minutes.

The opposing team was … the Chicago Cubs.

McGill would fit right in with the majority of the fans, rooting for the Nationals.

There was a polite knock at the suite's door. Deke answered it. Talked for a moment with the visitor and then admitted him. The Secret Service special agent stepped out into the corridor. Leo took his refreshments out to a padded chair on the field side of the box. He'd watch the game from there, and make sure no one tried to approach the suite from that side.

McGill stood and shook the newcomer's hand.

"Jim McGill," he said, introducing himself.

"Ben Holcomb."

The CIA officer was about McGill's height and age, slighter of build, but had a strong grip.

Further conversation was delayed by the playing of the National Anthem. As he always did, McGill sang along with the crowd. So did Holcomb. Surprising McGill a bit by his participation and more than a little by the quality of his voice. The man sang in a fine, clear tenor.

McGill complimented him on it after the country had been reaffirmed once more as the home of the brave.

Holcomb told McGill that his father was the choir master at

their church in Syracuse.

McGill asked if his guest would like anything to eat or drink. Holcomb said he was good.

They watched the first batter, the Cubs' right fielder, hit a blistering line drive that the Nationals' shortstop leaped high and caught in the web of his glove. The crowd came to its feet, cheering. McGill took that as an opportune moment to begin his conversation with Holcomb. Everyone else's attention, except Leo's, was on the field.

"My Secret Service agent checked this suite for listening devices," McGill told Holcomb. "He didn't find anything. We can speak freely."

"Your man is an expert at that task?"

"Yeah. You'd be surprised by how many people would like to know what I have to say."

"Maybe not," Holcomb said. "I'm here because several of the poobahs at Langley want to know what you have on your mind."

"Well, a little Russian girl by the name of Anya Ivanova wants me to find her lost dog, Misha. Offered me three days' pay to find him. I didn't take the money but I've started looking for the dog."

Holcomb said, "You know Anya's mother is on staff at the Russian Embassy?"

"I do."

"And you didn't think it might be a good idea to politely decline the case?"

"I have two daughters," McGill said. "I'm a sucker for little girls in need of help."

Holcomb offered a thin smile. "From what I've heard, you're not a sucker for anything."

"Okay, but I do have my sentimental moments."

"And maybe an ulterior motive?"

"We'll get to that," McGill said. "What I've found out so far is it's unlikely Misha was gobbled up by a coyote, and someone at the Chinese Embassy is looking for a dog of the same breed as Misha. Only they call it ZuZu."

Holcomb said, "Maybe the Chinese dog is an entrée on the lam."

McGill smiled. "My Secret Service special agent suggested as much. But I think Misha, aka ZuZu, served another purpose. Running messages between the Russians and the Chinese. What do you think of that idea?"

"Low tech but probably effective," Holcomb said.

"Exactly. I told the president I won't ask what surveillance methods our people apply to foreign embassies in Washington, but I'd bet it involves all sorts of sophisticated electronics and computers."

Holcomb had no comment.

McGill said, "Anyway, it occurred to me that the way to defeat modern surveillance would be by going old school. Use a dog as a courier, just like they did in World War One. But somebody on our side spotted Misha for what he is. Then someone else, higher up the food chain, decided to dognap Misha, see what they could glean by examining the poor little beast. Please tell me that he didn't expire while being questioned."

Holcomb looked at McGill for several seconds.

"You know, sir, you present quite a problem for us," he said.

McGill laughed. "You should hear what the Secret Service has to say."

There was another cheer from the crowd, and the home team came up to bat.

After the din died away when the batter touched home plate, Holcomb sighed and told McGill, "I've been cleared to use my judgment as to how much I can tell you."

"In other words, you hold your own rope. Use too little, you strangle slowly; use too much, you pop your head clean off."

"Hangman metaphors are so comforting," Holcomb said.

"So take solace in this: The only person I'll ever tell is the president, and she can find out on her own what's going on."

That did reassure the CIA man. Gave him a neat rationale to

use on his bosses, if need be. Because if McGill could tell the president, then she could tell him. One way or another, he could find out.

"We've got the dog," Holcomb said.

"Alive and well?"

"It's been sedated and exposed to some x-rays. Otherwise, yes."

"Did you find what you were looking for?"

"No."

McGill had spent an hour before going to the ballpark talking with Edwina Byington's son, the veterinarian and her granddaughter, the dog breeder.

He asked Holcomb, "What were you looking for, encoded information in the dog's microchip?"

It turned out dogs, some of them, weren't entirely analog technology.

Many of the critters came with microchips the size of a grain of rice. The purpose for the chips was to provide information on the dog's identity and the place it called home. That and the people who had taken responsibility for its welfare.

Holcomb didn't look surprised that McGill had made a good guess.

"That was one idea," he said.

"There were others?"

"We thought there might be a second chip, tucked in somewhere your average vet wouldn't think to put it. That's why we did the x-rays."

McGill nodded, as if he'd thought of that, too.

"You look for tattoos?" McGill asked.

"Yeah, that and even micro-inscription on the dog's teeth."

That hadn't occurred to McGill.

"So you came up with zilch, but you still think the dog's a messenger."

"Yeah," Holcomb said. "You got any ideas?"

"One."

"High tech?"

"Unh-uh. You ever hear the story about how our space program and the Russians' program set about solving the problem of writing in zero gravity?" McGill asked.

"Yeah, I know that one," Holcomb said. "NASA spent millions to create a pen; the Russians used a pencil."

"That's sort of what they did in this case, too, I think."

He explained his idea to the CIA man.

"Sonofabitch," Holcomb said.

"You're welcome," McGill said. "If you're careful, maybe the Russians and the Chinese won't figure out you're on to them. I won't take any money from the government for my assistance, but if you want to show some appreciation, make sure Anya gets her dog back."

He told Holcomb how to do that.

The president was still at work in the Oval Office when McGill's call was put through to her.

"Are you still laboring on behalf of the American electorate?" he asked.

"After five," she said, "I work only for the people who voted for me."

McGill laughed.

"Aren't you still at work?" she asked.

"I'm at the ball game. I can get you a beer, fast food and maybe even something with actual nutritional value, if you'd care to join me. It's still early innings."

"You think I can sneak away to a ball game?"

"I was asking myself that question. Is it possible for the president of the United States to sneak into a major league baseball game without being noticed? I decided if any historical figure could do it, you could."

The president said, "Let's find out."

Nobody actually saw the president enter the stadium, but her platoon of Secret Service agents didn't go unnoticed. By inference, it was soon known who was on the premises. Patricia Grant's likeness was shown on the Jumbotron. Beneath it, the number of people in attendance went up by one. The crowd came to its feet and gave a spontaneous cheer.

The manager of each team had the *savoir faire* to stand on the top step of his dugout, doff his cap and bow in the direction of the luxury suites.

McGill handed Patti a beer and a hot dog.

"Warms your heart, doesn't it?" he asked.

"It does indeed."

After a minute, the game resumed play.

McGill and the president had matters other than the game to occupy their minds.

"You found the dog?" she asked.

"The CIA has him."

"He's going to be repatriated?"

"So I'm told. If not, I thought you might twist some arms."

"I can do that, but I don't think that will be necessary."

"I command such implicit power?" McGill asked.

"It's not a secret we're a close couple. You're well liked, and it's generally known you don't throw your weight around without good reason."

"Even then, I don't do it often, preferring guile as I do."

"That and blarney," the president said.

"And a steely stare."

"Maybe a little gift, too, to ease their feelings?" the president asked.

"I told the CIA how I think the Russians and Chinese are transmitting messages."

"Their means of conniving being?"

"Something I noticed the other night at Montrose Park. The prevailing ethic of being a good dog owner in the nicer parts of town requires you to pick up after your pooch."

"You mean ..."

"There's a special waste can just for doggy-doo."

The president wrinkled her nose and said, "Yuck."

"I think that reaction is what the other side is counting on," McGill said. "But what the heck? The collection of night-soil has a long history; I looked it up. In the dog parks, the poop is tied up in plastic bags. That has to mitigate the stink somewhat. If you tie some sort of marker into the knot of the bag you want your opposite number to receive, that would make the job relatively easy."

"I can see you've given the matter considerable thought," Patti said, "but how do you get the dog to eat the capsule or microchip or whatever you use to send your message?"

McGill said, "Wrap it in braised beef. From what I saw first hand, there isn't a dog in the world that wouldn't eat plutonium if you wrapped it in braised beef."

Patti sighed. "If you've got it right, that means the Russians or Chinese have figured out how long it takes a dog to *process* the vessel carrying the message."

"I think so," McGill said.

"But neither side's diplomats would do the initial pickup."

"No, they're paying off local labor for that, I'd say."

"But what is it the Russians and Chinese are telling each other? Why not just talk to each other in Moscow or Beijing?" Patti asked.

"Must have something to do with their activities right here. In any case, that's above my pay grade. Once the CIA insinuates itself into the supply chain, they'll have to figure out a way to keep things going without the other side finding out, see what they're up to and tell you."

"Ah, the glamour of being the president," the president said.

McGill told her, "There is one other thing, of course."

"The Russians and the Chinese were testing you."

"Right. They wanted to see if I'm the kind of sap they can use to embarrass you. What with the political situation in Congress being so uncertain, they could really gum up the works here in Washington if they caused a scandal for you by having me take money from them and then, oops, something embarrassing, not to mention untrue, about my role gets leaked to the press."

"Leaving them to pursue their agendas around the world while we're too busy and at odds with each other to object. But you were smart enough not to take any money."

"Right, and I'm sure not going to return poor little Misha."

Patti looked at McGill. "Then who is?"

Georgi Travkin asked, "Do you want a reward?"

Steve Nagy shook his head. "That's all the reward I need."

He nodded toward Anya, who was down on her knees, clasping Misha to her chest, petting him top to bottom. Trying to feel if the American had implanted their own microchip in her dog. In the distance, Irina Ivanova, Anya's mother, held a camera with a telephoto lens and took pictures of the little gathering in Montrose Park. She'd hoped to get a nice group shot with McGill accepting a check from Georgi.

All they had for their efforts, though, were shots of some ordinary fellow refusing Georgi's offer of money. She could overhear them through the microphone in Georgi's tie-pin. Irina had no doubt the fellow was McGill's agent. Maybe someone in the American intelligence apparatus, maybe a personal friend. Whoever he was, he'd been paid something to play his part.

He was a handsome fellow, and his dog was magnificent.

Who knew, maybe he was the type who liked foreign women.

Irina would have to see.

The three Russians and their dog reunited at the Mercedes sedan that Georgi would use to drive them to the embassy. They weren't happy with the ways things had gone; the Chinese were certain to laugh at their failed effort. Still, there was no great cause for distress.

The Americans were in disarray and —

Georgi drew his gun and told Anya and Irina to step back.

He took a deep breath and yanked open the backseat driver-side door.

Then he looked at Irina and Anya and said, "Дерьмо."

Shit.

Irina nudged Georgi out of the way. She and Anya looked inside.

On the backseat lay a box of Milkbone dog biscuits.

There was no card with it.

Even so, they all knew it came from McGill.

Pins & Needles

McGill Short Case #3

The National Football League took its cues from *Carcharodon carcharias,* the great white shark. It never stopped moving and it consumed the audiences of lesser sport leagues. Unlike the terror of the ocean, though, the NFL did not have to hunt. Once the league opened its maw, vast numbers of Americans voluntarily stuffed it with their money and their rapt attention.

McGill was one of them. To a somewhat lesser degree than most.

He willingly paid the premium that was added to his cable TV bill to cover the cost of televising pro football. He bought sweatshirts for himself and his son, Kenny, with their favorite team's logo on them. He played catch with Kenny using the league's official ball.

But McGill didn't attend games in person. The prices for tickets were outrageous, and he considered the advent of the personal seat license, the fee required for the right to buy season tickets, to be nothing short of extortion. He had it in the back of his mind that if his wife, the president of the United States, ever had an idle moment, he'd ask her to have the Department of Justice open a criminal investigation into the practice.

In any case, football was a game he preferred to watch on television. You always had the best seat in the house. You never had to worry about rain or frostbite. Replays from many angles clarified close calls. And you never had to stand in line to use a urinal.

Back in the old days, pro football had been a seasonal sport, early to late fall with maybe just a toehold on winter. The league played a championship game in December and that was it. See you next year, everybody.

Then came the Super Bowl. The first one was played on January 15, 1967. So a season that had begun in one year was completed in another. By 2013, the Super Bowl had been pushed back to February third. The NFL draft, that year, had become a three-day must-see TV event in April; in 2014 the draft would move to May. The Hall of Fame exhibition game, the first of the preseason, would be played on August fourth. The hunger of the great white shark grew endlessly.

If there was one part of the calendar the league had yet to swallow whole it was late June, after organized team activities had ended and before training camp began in July. Doubtless, the league was making plans for that fallow period, but on the third Monday in June the only sports related question McGill had on his mind was whether he might live long enough to see the Chicago White Sox win another World Series.

That was when Sweetie poked her head into McGill's office and asked him, "How big did you say that guy in France was, the one you and your friends fought under the bridge?"

He knew immediately whom she meant: Etienne Burel, aka The Undertaker.

"Over seven feet tall and better than four hundred pounds."

"Okay, well, we have someone here to see you who's not quite that big but he's pretty close."

McGill gave that a moment's thought. Sweetie wasn't in the least agitated, so however big the guy in the outer office might be, his demeanor had to be peaceful for the moment. That was good. McGill hoped his days of fighting giants with sticks were over.

"Did he say what he wants?"

"He'd like you to find a woman for him."

McGill's eyes widened. That had been his exact task in Paris.

Then again, missing persons were something of a stock-in-trade for private investigators.

He asked, "Why does he want to find the woman?"

Sweetie looked over her shoulder and then back to McGill.

"I'd like to hear that myself," she said. "He's got a friend with him. You want to see them?"

McGill wasn't sure that he *wanted* to see them, but he said, "Okay."

The big guy was Matthew Mingo, the first round draft choice of the NFL's Washington franchise. McGill remembered reading about him in the sports section of the *Post*. He was an offensive left tackle, the lineman who protected a right-handed quarterback from getting smashed from his blind side. As such, his position was highly valued in football's scheme of things, and left tackles were paid accordingly if they were any good.

If McGill recalled the young man's published measurements right, he stood six-foot-ten and weighed three hundred and eighty pounds. Not quite as big as Etienne Burel but close enough to be his kid brother. Unlike the French thug, Matthew had an almost timorous air about him. Like he was afraid someone was going to jump out of a shadow and say, "Boo!" Make him scamper away and hide.

Not exactly a temperament held in high esteem by pro scouts.

With the young giant was the team's general manager, Henry Harker, the man responsible for drafting Matthew and making him an instant millionaire. Harker's eyes also held a glint of anxiety. Like maybe he'd just made the worst and perhaps final mistake of his career. Unlike Matthew, though, the way Harker carried himself was aggressive. His shoulders were squared and his hands were clenched.

Sweetie made the introductions.

Showing deference to age and status, McGill shook Harker's

hand first. The man couldn't help himself; he gave McGill's hand a good squeeze. McGill met it with equal pressure and kept his smile in the process. When he shook Matthew's hand, the would-be pro went easy, but McGill could sense the amount of power he held in reserve.

Woe betide any fool on defense who tried to bull-rush young Matthew Mingo.

McGill didn't have a chair that would hold Matthew. Even Harker would be a tight fit. That being the case, McGill suggested they go downstairs and have a cool drink in the shade of one of Dikki Missirian's café umbrellas. Assuming Matthew would fit under one.

Harker said, "If you don't mind, Mr. McGill, I'd just as soon we keep this private. We don't want another team getting a scouting report on what we have to say here today."

The general manager gave Sweetie a look. She held it and smiled at him.

McGill said, "Ms. Sweeney is a partner in this firm. If you don't feel comfortable talking with her, and listening to any expert advice she might have for you, you'll need to look for help elsewhere."

Harker sighed and nodded.

"I stand by my people, too. I respect what you're saying. Could I maybe get something to drink?"

"Soft drink or sparkling water?" Sweetie asked.

"I could use some caffeine," Harker said.

Sweetie gently put a hand on Matthew's arm. He almost jumped.

He made himself relax, and Sweetie asked, "How about you?"

"Water, ma'am. Thank you."

McGill heard a note of Caribbean creole with an overlay of the American South in the young man's voice. His skin color, light cocoa, and eyes, hazel, pointed to a multiethnic heritage. Sweetie was back in a moment with three bottles of sparkling Poland Spring and a cola for Harker.

She and McGill leaned against his desk.

Their prospective clients stood and faced them.

"So what's the problem?" McGill asked.

Harker said, "You know, I thought I'd seen it all in football."

"But?" McGill asked.

"But this fine young man standing next to me, someone who should play fifteen years before he goes into the Hall of Fame, someone I'm on the hook to for twenty million dollars in guaranteed money ... he went and got himself on the wrong side of a voodoo queen."

McGill and Sweetie looked at each other.

Then they looked at Matthew Mingo.

He nodded in confirmation of Harker's claim.

Matthew told his story.

"Maman gave me up for adoption in Port-au-Prince. I was ten years old. Hard as she worked, she couldn't make enough money to keep me fed. I've always eaten a lot. I told Maman, though, I'd eat only one meal a day, if she'd keep me. We tried that for a while, but it didn't work. I was so hungry by the time I ate that only meal I had to beg for more.

"That broke Maman's heart, she told me. Made her cry to think she couldn't do right for me. I told her I'd try to get by on what she could give me. I made sure she didn't hear me complain one little bit. Only way I could do that, though, was to steal food from other people. At first, I robbed our neighbors. I was already so big nobody tried to stop me. What stopped me was hearing other kids cry from going hungry 'cause I stole their food. I knew how it felt to be hungry all the time, so I couldn't do that any more.

"I started stealing from trucks that brought mangos, bananas, oranges and cashews to market. At first, I just stole for myself, what I could eat. It wasn't hard. People saw how big I was were scared to try and stop me. Some of the men were as big as I was then, but none of them could catch me when I took to running. For the first time I could remember, I wasn't hungry.

"That was also the first time I noticed how skinny Maman was. So I started stealing food for her, too. That scared her. Not so bad that she didn't eat what I brought her. But she was sure I'd be caught, maybe beaten to death by thugs hired by the people I robbed. Maybe sent to prison if the police took an interest in catching me. Maman worried every day about bad things happening to me, but I could see she wasn't hungry now either, and that made me feel good.

"If I kept going, just robbing for the two of us, it might have worked out, but I got the idea of helping other people have enough to eat, too. I got some boys from the families I used to take food from and they helped me steal from the trucks. That was when I went too far. Men with guns came and beat Maman when I wasn't home. Said they'd kill her if she didn't help them catch me."

Matthew paused to fight back tears.

"I was playing soccer with some of my boys on a ragged old field when the men with the guns came for me. Maman told them where they could find me. But she'd also told me they'd be coming. I thought she was just trying to scare me, saying that, get me to stop stealing from the trucks. When my boys and me saw those men we ran like the devil was after us.

"Maman had told me where I should go, a fine hotel on the beach where only people from America and Europe could afford to stay. Funny thing was, I had to hide in the kitchen when I got there. The cooks fed me. They gave me a hamburger, and I'd never tasted anything so good. I swallowed it in three bites and then licked my fingers for ten minutes.

"Wasn't too longer before a man and woman came in and looked at me. They were white and both of them were bigger than me. I thought they were going to take me to the police or the men with the guns. I told them how sorry I was. I promised never to steal or do anything wrong again. I begged them to take me back to Maman.

"That was when the woman smiled at me and said, 'I'm your new mama.' She showed me a piece of paper she said was from

Maman giving the man and woman permission to adopt me."

Matthew couldn't keep the tears from falling now.

Sweetie gave him a tissue from the box in McGill's desk.

Matthew composed himself and continued. "I didn't want to be adopted. But the man said they would take me to America and they would give me all the food I could eat. The woman said they would send money to Maman, too, so she wouldn't be hungry either.

"When the man and woman said they wouldn't let the men with the guns get me, I went. My new parents adopted me officially in Louisiana, and Mathieu became Matthew.

"I started school in Baton Rouge, they wouldn't let me play football with the other kids because I was too big. I would've hurt somebody. I couldn't even play soccer, not forward, midfield or defense, for the same reason. But they let me play goalkeeper."

A smile of fond remembrance lit his face. "Man, wasn't anybody who could score on me. I had quick feet. I'd spread my arms wide and any little kid on the other team would see me and think not only was I gonna block his shot, I was gonna gobble him up for dinner."

That was when Harker said, "That's just what I want the teams we play to think about Matthew when they line up against us."

McGill thought that was a little optimistic.

Of course, if Matthew's game-face ever matched his size, maybe not.

He continued his narrative. "I played soccer right through high school. Made all-state. I was happy being in sports because that was how I made all my friends. I was really big by then, but people weren't scared of me. I never felt so happy in my life. Only thing was, I didn't have a girlfriend."

"Because of your size not your color," Sweetie said.

"Mostly because of my size. Some people liked me all right when I was playing. Not as much before or after a match."

"Okay," Harker said, "now tell them about Hilaire."

Matthew nodded. "I went to LSU on a football scholarship. My soccer coach told the football coach at LSU about me. Coach said if I played football I would have the chance to bang against other guys who were almost my size. That made me smile, just the idea of it. Coach put me on the offensive line, told me to think of it like I was still a goalkeeper. The other team had eleven players. I had to think of each of them as a ball that was trying to get past me. My job was to stop one of them for sure. Maybe even two or three. If I could do that, I'd be rich and famous right after graduation.

"I did pretty good," Matthew said, smiling for the first time.

McGill now remembered how well he'd done.

"You were All-American, right?"

Matthew nodded. "Won the Rotary Lombardi Award, too."

The prize for the top college lineman on offense or defense.

"And then Hilaire came along?" McGill asked.

"After freshman season, the team went out to dinner in New Orleans to celebrate our accomplishments and set goals for next year. After dinner, we were free to go our own ways, but coach said, 'Don't none of y'all get yourselfs arrested.'"

"Did you," Sweetie asked, "get arrested?"

"No, ma'am. My Mama Louise and Daddy Lyle told me I had no choice in life but to stand out, and I should do it for somethin' good, not somethin' bad. I never forgot that — and I don't never want any men with guns coming after me again."

"So what did you do?" McGill asked.

"I went out to hear some music and see the sights."

McGill said, "Did you do any drinking?"

"I don't drink alcohol at all, and I don't do no drugs."

"All that leaves is someone pretty," Sweetie said.

"Yes, ma'am. That was the night I met Hilaire. I was sitting by myself outside a little café, sippin' my ice tea. She sat down at the table like we knew each other forever and she'd just come back from the ladies' room."

"What'd she have to say?" McGill asked.

Matthew blushed. "She said I had more handsome on me than all the stars in Hollywood and half the angels in heaven."

Sweetie said, "Give her points for originality."

"She wasn't hard to look at either, was she?" McGill asked.

"No, sir. Not at all."

Sweetie said, "What happened next?"

"She asked if she could see my right hand."

"Your palm?"

"Both sides. She looked at my hand, ran her fingertips over it, sent chills right up my spine. Then she put both her hands over mine, and I felt warm, like gettin' into a hot bath on a cold night. She smiled at me and said she saw great things in my future ... but I wasn't quite ready for her yet."

McGill said, "Did you think you were ready for her that night?"

Matthew's face darkened more than before.

"I was ready to jump over the moon for her. But she said no, and both my mamas taught me to always behave myself with ladies. Hilaire told me she knew all the mysteries of life and could see the future. Even better, she would help me make the right choices in my life. If I had a big question that needed to be answered, I could ask her for advice."

"Did you ask for her help?" Sweetie asked.

"I called her once a month. That was all she would allow. I told her about school and being on the football team. She always said I should be respectful of authority."

"Did you ever ask her about your social life?" Sweetie said.

Matthew looked down, needed a long moment before he could answer.

"I asked her about some girls I'd met, yes ma'am."

Sweetie told him, "She said you'd be better off without them."

Matthew only nodded.

"She never wanted any money for her advice, did she?" McGill said.

"No, sir. Not until later."

"Shortly after you were drafted to play in the NFL?"

"Yes, sir."

"Right about the time the media announced what you'd get paid," Sweetie said.

"Yes, ma'am. Right after that."

Harker said, "Tell them why we're here, Matthew."

"When I told her I wouldn't give her half my money, that was when I started to hurt."

Harker took things from there.

"The league and the players' association have a symposium for rookies each year. The purpose is to educate our youngest players on what it means to become a professional athlete, the privileges and the pitfalls. Many of these guys find themselves with more money in their pockets and bank accounts than they ever could have imagined. In too many cases, they run through small fortunes before their playing days are over.

"We try to help them understand that a million dollars or even several million isn't all the money in the world. You can burn through it so fast you don't even know how it got spent — or in some cases stolen. Schemers, moochers and even armed robbers come after players. These young men might be terrors on the field, but many of them are soft touches for their old friends and just plain naive when it comes to women.

"So part of the program has to do with the responsible management of the money they're getting paid. In a lot of cases, the classes might as well be taught in Greek, but Matthew's adoptive parents are successful small business people. Between their dry cleaning shops and laundromats, they operate a dozen locations. They're comfortably situated financially and they showed Matthew how it all works: revenues, expenses, taxes and net income. He knew just what he was hearing at the symposium. Don't let any sharp dealers try to take your money away from you. Keep a close eye on your spending. Live within your means.

"When Hilaire demanded half of his income, he knew just what to say: No."

"I did offer to buy her some new clothes," Matthew said.

Harker smiled. "Items with less décolletage."

"She's pretty enough without showing so much," Matthew said. "But she didn't like that either. She said she'd been giving me the advice for three years that made me an honors student and the football player that got drafted so high, and she wanted half my contract and not a penny less."

"So you said no again," Sweetie said.

"Yes, ma'am."

"And she did what?" McGill asked. "Put a curse on you?"

"Showed me this doll she'd made. Looks just like me. Wearing my Washington uniform, without the helmet. It was for anything else, I'd like to have one. But she stuck a pin in the doll's right knee, and I got an awful pain in the same spot. All but dropped me to the ground."

"Did you think of grabbing the doll from her?" McGill asked.

"I did, but I thought what if she makes another."

"Did you think of showing her she could get hurt, too?" Sweetie asked.

Matthew shook his head. "No, ma'am. I've never hit anyone off a football field in my life, especially a woman. Like I said, my mamas were real clear about that. The league was, too. You can't play football or do much else in a jail cell."

"What did you do?" McGill asked.

"I walked out on Hilaire, not saying another word, doing my best not to limp. Wasn't easy. My leg hurt like it was on fire."

Harker said, "It's not always Matthew's knees. Sometimes it's other joints: hips, ankles, shoulders."

"You look into early onset arthritis?" McGill asked.

"It's not always joints. Sometimes it's headaches, rapid heart beat, intestinal distress. We've had internists, orthopedist, rheumatologists, more doctors than I ever heard of look at Matthew," Harker said. "All the tests come back negative."

McGill and Sweetie glanced at each other.

"Has Matthew seen a psychologist?" McGill asked.

The general manager gestured to his new player.

"Yes, sir. I spent three hours talking to Doctor Sandra Valenzuela. She says I'm well adjusted. Only thing maybe is wrong with me, I'm too suggestible. I didn't know what that meant until she told me."

"You take to heart ideas you should ignore," Sweetie said.

"Yes, ma'am. It's something I just can't help, I guess."

McGill looked at Harker and asked, "What is it you think Ms. Sweeney and I might do for you and Matthew, Mr. Harker?"

He said, "It was Doctor Valenzuela who gave me the idea. She thinks you should steal Hilaire's juju. Not the doll, just the magic."

McGill and Sweetie were struck speechless. Momentarily.

Then both of them began to smile. Each was sure there was no law against stealing juju, not that they'd ever heard of. Even if there was, how could such a thing be proven? Doctor Valenzuela surely knew she was suggesting a psychological ploy.

McGill and Sweetie found the idea elegant.

There was just one more thing McGill wanted to know.

He asked Harker, "Does your team play the Chicago Bears this season?"

"Unh-uh, they're not on our schedule."

"Okay, we'll give it a try," McGill said.

It would have been hard for him to make it possible for Matthew to abuse his favorite team.

On his way out, Harker gave McGill his business card.

That and mention Hilaire was in town, staying at The Willard.

Right up the street from the White House, McGill thought.

Leo drove McGill and Sweetie to the White House, after making a quick stop at The Willard. The manager assured McGill that the esteemed hotel, while having suites named after Washington, Jefferson, Adams and Lincoln, had no Voodoo Queen suite. Responding to the question of whether Ms. Hilaire DeVary was still a guest, McGill was told such information was confidential.

McGill said, "I'll check with the *Washington Post* to see if the story has leaked yet."

For just a moment a flicker of worry appeared in the man's eyes.

As if trouble might have come to his hotel.

Telling McGill that Hilaire was still in the building.

Moving along to the White House, McGill asked the president's personal secretary, Edwina Byington, if it would be all right if he and Sweetie used the president's personal library. Permission was granted, with the understanding that he could get Google elsewhere in the building, if he chose.

Reading between the lines, he understood he shouldn't go peeking into top secret stuff.

McGill had always been good about that; not knowing presidential secrets made for more peaceful sleep. He didn't want to use the room for poking his nose where it didn't belong. He wanted it because it was off limits to more people than even his Hideaway. You could work there without interruption.

Also, he suspected Google and the other civilian search engines tried to curry favor with the president by giving her faster and more thorough searches than your average Joe got.

He and Sweetie entered the room.

She looked around and said, "Nice, has a sense of self-restraint."

As a young woman, Sweetie had once lived in a convent.

Her sense of self-indulgence was a mint on the pillow.

"Let's see what we can find out about sticking needles in dolls," McGill said, pulling a chair up to the gleaming iMac that Patti used as her spyglass on the world. Among its more mundane functions, it could be used the way earlier generations turned to encyclopedias. McGill keyed in: sympathetic magic.

He was referred to imitative magic.

Sweetie pulled up a chair at McGill's right shoulder.

"Somebody always has to come along and put their own imprint on things," she said.

"Uh-huh." McGill found the screen he was looking for, and the two former Chicago cops read in silence. After a number of page changes and about thirty minutes, they'd learned enough for their purposes. McGill returned the computer to the browser's start page and left the history of their search in place, in case Patti cared to see what they were up to.

McGill and Sweetie pushed their chairs back from the desk.

They swiveled them so they were facing each other.

"I didn't know you had such a handle on this stuff," Sweetie said. "Knowing right where to look on the Internet."

"Got it from Kenny. He loves that zombie show on cable TV. Voodoo is the next-door neighbor to zombie-land."

"Educational television, huh? So the whole point of imitative magic is you use a symbolic object, a fetish if you want to be high-brow, to affect real people."

"Stick the doll's knee, make Matthew's leg hurt," McGill said.

"He has to buy into the whole idea. He sees Hilaire stick the doll, he knows he's *supposed* to hurt in the corresponding place."

McGill said, "We don't know all the circumstances of his early life in Haiti; maybe he was raised that way."

"Could be," Sweetie said, "but seeing someone stick a doll that looks like you is one thing. The symbolic violence takes place right in front of your eyes and triggers real pain. But how does she hurt Matthew when the two of them aren't in the same place?"

McGill thought about that.

After a minute, he said, "She phones it in?"

Sweetie said, "No, *he* calls her. Remember what Matthew said: He'd have jumped over the moon for her."

"All the girls like bad boys, and all the boys like bad girls?" McGill asked.

"If Hilaire really managed to keep Matthew from getting seriously involved with any other girls, who does that leave him to think about?"

McGill elaborated. "Fantasize about. His voodoo queen. Maybe the fact that she has power over him is its own kind of turn-on."

Sweetie wrinkled her nose.

"I know," McGill said, "it's not for me either, but different strokes for different folks."

Sweetie remembered just how *different* people could be from her days as a patrol cop.

"Yeah, I suppose. We'll need to check Matthew's phone records. See who he's called."

"Or," McGill said, "just ask him. The kid doesn't exactly have a poker face."

Sweetie laughed. "No, he doesn't. You know what I have to wonder, though. What we're dealing with here, in modern medical terms, is the placebo effect. So how come nobody uses these fetishes for beneficial purposes? You know, if you've got a fever, you stick the doll in the freezer and you're well again."

McGill grinned. "I think there is something like that in folk medicine. I'll have to check with Kenny and —"

He sat still, looking at but no longer seeing Sweetie.

She gave him a moment before asking, "You have a big idea or a small stroke?"

"Idea," McGill said, coming back into focus. "Did you see the reference to corresponding healing in the material we read?"

"Yeah," Sweetie said. "Where does that get us?"

McGill rolled his chair back to the iMac's keyboard.

Pulled up the information he sought.

He read to Sweetie, "Certain herbs with yellow sap can cure jaundice, walnuts can strengthen the brain because of their resemblance to it and phallic-shaped roots can ... well, do what Viagra does at a fraction of the cost."

Sweetie said, "And from all that you came up with?"

"How we're going to cure Matthew, if Hilaire won't play ball."

McGill gave Sweetie the details.

She smiled and said, "I like it."

"Voodoo?" Patti said, "Really?"

She'd just entered her White House bedroom. McGill was already in bed. He paused the on-demand movie he'd been watching, *The Serpent and the Rainbow*. Strange doings in Haiti. Forces of good and evil, science and magic.

Patti had glanced at the still image on the television and identified the movie immediately.

McGill said, "I didn't think you'd know it. The movie was shot back in the '80s. You must have been a child when you saw it."

Patti laughed, something that didn't happen often enough in any president's day.

"Your blarney is just what I need," she said, sitting on the bed next to him.

"Something you can share?" McGill asked.

There was a lot that she couldn't.

"Representative Philip Brock, Democrat of Pennsylvania, I wouldn't mind having someone stick pins in him, and not just symbolically."

"Causing trouble, is he?"

"Trying hard. If his idea catches on, he could turn the country upside down."

"What does he want to do?"

Patti said, "Convene a constitutional convention, open the whole constitution to a rewrite."

McGill grimaced. "As divided as the country is right now, that could lead to chaos."

"I think that's just what the gleeful SOB wants. The problem is, the idea has appeal to both ends of the political spectrum. Each side would *love* to see the country remade in its image."

"So the question is: Can the center hold?" McGill said.

"That's it, all right. You really want to watch the rest of the movie?"

"Does the good guy win?" McGill asked.

"Yes. There was no keeping him down." Patti headed to her bathroom. "I'll be out in five minutes."

McGill clicked off the TV and turned out the lights.

He caught Patti's double entendre. You couldn't keep a zombie down. Same could be said for a good man. Things came to a showdown between the two, McGill knew where he'd put his money.

McGill called the Washington GM, Henry Harker, from his office at nine a.m. He'd read many times that pro football execs and coaches worked an ungodly number of hours each day, but he didn't want to call early and find out that was a bunch of hooey. Even at his age, McGill liked to cling to an illusion or two.

Harker came on the phone and got right to the point.

"You get Hilaire to back off yet?"

McGill said, "Still working on the game plan. A thought came to me this morning. Why wasn't Matthew's agent with the two of you yesterday? Seems like he should have an interest in the situation, too."

"He did. The wrong interest. The guy wanted Matthew to let him negotiate with Hilaire. Said he was sure he could get her to lower her demand from fifty percent."

"Wait a minute," McGill said. "What's this agent's name?"

"Cyrus Zale."

"And he wanted to pay off an extortionist?"

"Zale said the cops couldn't do anything; there aren't any laws against sticking pins in a doll."

"None that I've heard of," McGill agreed. "Did Matthew dump the guy?"

"His contract with Zale didn't allow for an early termination without a stiff buyout penalty." Harker laughed. "So what the kid did, and I love him for it, he told Zale to give Hilaire one hundred percent of his commission."

"Zale gets what, three percent of Matthew's contract value?" McGill asked.

"Right. That's all the league allows."

"Did Zale give Matthew an estimate of how much he could reduce Hilaire's demand?"

"Yeah. He said he was sure he could get her to knock it down by half."

McGill laughed. "So he was willing to negotiate a deal that would give Hilaire more than eight times what he was earning. Sounds like he was working for her more than his client. That or Hilaire is just a front for him. But Zale didn't go for Matthew's suggestion, did he?"

"No, he didn't. That was when Matthew leaned over him and told him if he didn't take his offer to Hilaire, then Matthew would take him to court, and it would be the worst day of Zale's life if the judge actually saw things Zale's way."

McGill remembered the enormous, if restrained, strength in Matthew's handshake.

Wouldn't be a good idea to get someone like him mad at you.

"So Zale said he and Matthew should go their separate ways, and nothing in their contract kept him from bailing out early," McGill said.

"You got it," Harker told him.

McGill took a moment to think things through.

Then he told Harker, "I need you to do a couple things to help me."

"Like what?" There was a note of reluctance in the GM's voice.

"I need the names of every other player in the league represented by Zale."

"I can't do that. I told you we want to keep the other teams from learning our situation."

Harker certainly had, and now McGill understood why.

"You remember I asked you if your team plays the Bears this season?" McGill asked.

"Yeah."

"I did that because I wouldn't want to see Washington beat Chicago. You, on the other hand, don't want to see any team beat Washington. That's understandable for you. But it's not acceptable to me. You know Zale's got other clients playing in the league and they're not going to be at their best if they're worried about Hilaire. That gives you a competitive advantage."

"Yeah, it does. I hope you also figured out that some of Zale's other clients play for teams that are on Chicago's schedule this year."

McGill had thought of that. He sighed. "So we'll both have to suck it up. I get the names of Zale's other clients or my business relationship with you is over. There's no early-out penalty in our agreement."

Harker offered to double McGill's fee to do things his way.

McGill said he couldn't be bought.

Harker gave in, grumbling.

"One more thing," McGill said. "E-mail me a picture of Hilaire. If you don't have one, Matthew certainly does. The sooner I get it the better."

The GM sent him a headshot of Hilaire within a minute.

Quite the looker, McGill thought. Older than Matthew but still fetching enough to seize the young giant's imagination if not his bank balance. Put her up against other young athletes who liked to drink and do recreational pharmaceuticals, and lacked Matthew's understanding of personal wealth, she was sure to come out on top most if not all of the time.

Leaving her victims blindsided and broke.

McGill called Sweetie. Told her about Cyrus Zale.

Forwarded Hilaire's picture to her.

Sweetie picked up Hilaire coming out of The Willard. The hotel doorman smiled ear to ear for the simple pleasure of admitting her to the great outdoors. Sweetie thought the guy might brighten his day further by ushering her into a town car, but Hilaire was out for a stroll. She headed off in the direction of the nearby White House.

Sweetie got out of her classic Chevy Malibu, renewed the time on her parking meter and fell into step behind Hilaire. The first thing Sweetie noticed was the woman had a nice spring in her step, a good sense of balance, too, to keep her stride smooth in three-inch heels. Dark hair, straightened and colored with flecks of gold, fell to broad shoulders. Toned arms, a small waist, slim hips and long legs completed the physical picture from behind.

The dress she wore was gauzy and colorful, the hem an inch or two above her knees.

Sweetie had seen the style before. Thought it was called sea gypsy or something like that.

Wouldn't work for Sweetie. She was toned from a lifetime of

running and strength work, but her overall size and bone structure were wrong for something like that. Gauzy stuff just looked too precious on her. On the other hand, she looked great in close fitting cuts of sleek fabrics.

Putting thoughts of fashion aside, Sweetie watched for anyone approaching Hilaire. The Caribbean lady drew plenty of glances from oncoming pedestrians, both male and female. But no one said hello. Several people glanced over their shoulders to check out the rear view.

Sweetie thought Hilaire might have wanted to give a backward look or two herself. To remind the voyeurs not to be so overtly rude, if nothing else. Most women could sense when they were the subjects of unwanted attention. A voodoo queen certainly should have been mindful.

Hilaire was either unaware or indifferent.

Sweetie decided to test the woman. Close the distance between them. See when she finally appeared on Hilaire's radar, and if the woman could tell her interest was more than casual. She got to within ten feet of her target before she saw Hilaire's shoulders hunch just a bit.

Hilaire turned. The expression on her face showed she knew Sweetie was an adversary.

The two women stopped and faced each other directly opposite the White House.

Hilaire told Sweetie, "You don't want to be messin' with me, missy."

Unfazed, Sweetie asked, "You know who I am?"

"You someone I put a curse on real quick, you don't go away."

Hilaire's eyes were deeply set and dark with flecks of gold, just like her hair.

Contact lenses, Sweetie figured. But the woman's annoyance was real.

Sweetie laughed. "I'm curse-proof."

"We see about that."

"I'm not Matthew Mingo," Sweetie said,

That made Hilaire take a step back.

Sweetie continued, "And I've got a guardian angel. In fact, in some people's eyes, I am a guardian angel."

Hilaire started to murmur. Something in a threatening tone and a Creole tongue.

She stopped when Sweetie took out her phone and started shooting video.

"Sorry," Sweetie said. "I don't speak your language, but I'm sure I can get it translated. While you don't scare me, there is, in fact, a crime called menacing. Means you can't go around threatening people. Saying you're going to put a hurt or even a curse on them."

A sense of fear brightened Hilaire's eyes. Made the gold flecks sparkle. Maybe she wasn't wearing contacts. Didn't matter. This time she was the one getting the scare.

Before Hilaire could turn and run, Sweetie asked her, "Did you hear that Matthew told Zale he should give you his three percent of Matthew's contract?"

Hilaire didn't answer, not verbally. But the expression on her face told Sweetie that this was news to her. Now, Hilaire's impulse was not only to get away from Sweetie but also to confront Zale. That was easy for Sweetie to see, too.

She had a lot experience from her days as a cop, seeing bad guys fall out.

Still, she wasn't done with Hilaire quite yet.

"You want to forget about cursing me and listen for a minute," Sweetie said, "I know a way you might get more than just three percent from Zale."

She hadn't talked over her idea with Jim McGill yet, but she knew him.

He'd go along with it.

"What's in it for you?" Hilaire asked, suspicion in her voice.

"Only the satisfaction of doing the right thing," Sweetie said. "That's how I stay curse-proof."

***

McGill spent the rest of his day on the phone. Harker had given him a list of twenty-two other players in the league who were represented by Cyrus Zale. Each name came with a phone number.

"Can't swear all the numbers are current," Harker said.

"Why not?"

"Sometimes players prank each other by giving out teammates' numbers to the groupies."

McGill thought about that. "Targeting single guys for the gag, right? Wouldn't go over big if a married guy's wife answered his phone and heard from a strange woman."

"There have been locker room fights over things like that."

"Must be hard to keep the stars in line," McGill said.

"Only until you tell them they'd better not slip up, if they want to keep being jokesters."

"Has to be a hard life," McGill said, "playing pro football."

"Short and brutal, too," Harker replied. "You think you'll have this worked out soon?"

"Yeah, I've got the game plan in place now. No more than a day or two if I can get even half-a-dozen of these guys together with me."

"They need any special encouragement, let me know. I'll get my front office colleagues to add a little incentive."

Turned out that wasn't necessary.

McGill reached players at fourteen of the twenty-two numbers he called.

Twelve of them were all for his plan. That was plenty.

Add in Matthew Mingo, that gave him a baker's dozen.

Returning to the Executive Mansion, McGill called on Artemus Nicolaides, the White House physician. He told Nick, "I need the name of a specialist in New Orleans."

"You are feeling well?" Nick asked.

"Tiptop. This isn't for me."

McGill told Nick what he wanted and added, "If you can find someone who is ex-military, maybe been through a battle or two, that would be icing on the cake."

Not a problem. Nick didn't know anyone like that personally, but he knew a Cajun orthopedic surgeon in New Orleans who was friends with someone who fit the bill perfectly. After four-plus years of being married to the president, McGill was not surprised.

The first commandment at the White House was, "Thou shalt not disappoint."

Meaning the president, but McGill was allowed to ride her coattails.

Since they were working on an NFL team's dime, McGill and Sweetie flew to New Orleans first class. So did Deke and Leo, of course. In days gone by, business class would have been just fine. After traveling regularly on Air Force One, though, people tended to get spoiled.

Sweetie told McGill of her plan to assure Hilaire's presence — Zale's, too — and how she had thought to drive a wedge between the two of them.

He liked the idea, but asked, "You think the players will want to give up *any* of their money?"

"It was Matthew's idea, right?" Sweetie said. "I think they'll like this better than getting all their money back."

"You're probably right," McGill conceded. "I'll gather the guys up front, explain their options. Anybody who doesn't like it can go home with our apologies for bothering them."

Leo checked out the SUV the local office of the Secret Service brought to the airport and drove everyone to the Roosevelt Hotel. All the NFL players represented by Cyrus Zale were already in their rooms and joined McGill and Sweetie in his suite, as did J. R. Sullivan, the specialist Nick had found for McGill.

The hotel, befitting a five-star establishment, came up with a white board and black and red markers for McGill. He drew up the play so all the guys could envision their responsibilities and work together as a team.

McGill had booked an event space in the hotel called The Saenger Room. For a reception, the room had a maximum occupancy of twenty people. Eighteen would be present. Sweetie, Deke and himself plus the thirteen players and Hilaire and Zale.

McGill wanted the feeling to be cozy.

The players entered the room in business attire, as befitted the hotel's ambience. McGill explained to them what Sullivan's medical specialty was. He also told them Sullivan was a former army helicopter pilot in Operation Desert Storm, the first Persian Gulf war, and the winner of a Bronze Star with the V device awarded for heroism. The players doffed their street clothes and lined up before Sullivan wearing only gym shorts. The smallest player was half again bigger than Sullivan, but they all paid rapt attention to him as he told his stories of being a real warrior and went about his work.

When Sullivan finished he accepted a check from McGill and asked if he might stay and watch from the sidelines. McGill said, "Sure."

Nineteen in the room made it cozier still.

Everyone took his place, and McGill dimmed the lights.

Having timed things well, they needed to wait only a few minutes.

Hilaire led Cyrus Zale to The Saenger Room. She wore a Naeem Khan appliquéd cocktail dress in black and white. He wore a black Lanvin suit with a crimson tie. They were dressed up to do a night on the town, but first Hilaire had a surprise for Cyrus.

She let him worm it out of her.

"Matthew wants to see you," she told him.

Cyrus laughed. "I knew you'd scare him into coming back to me. Guys like that, they'll beat on each other 'til they drop. But a woman? She can scare them just like —"

Cyrus opened the door to The Saenger Room.

He was the one who shrieked.

Hilaire pushed him into the room and closed the door behind her. That was before *she* saw Matthew. He stood before them, monstrous in size, wearing only a pair of shorts and ...

Fine silvery needles sticking out of him everywhere.

His scalp, his face, his neck, his shoulders, arms and torso, his legs and feet.

Good God, there was even a needle in the inner corner of his right eye.

Cyrus turned to bolt from the room. Only now there was a man with a hard Afro-Eurasian face blocking the door. He was fully dressed. Even so, it was impossible to miss the outline of the weapon under his coat. Not just a handgun. It looked like a compact automatic weapon.

He didn't take it out. Didn't say a word. Doing either was unnecessary.

There would be no getting past him.

Things got even worse when another massive, multi-punctured figure stepped out of the shadows. Cyrus and Hilaire both recognized him. Another client, another sucker. A player who'd paid Cyrus his league-mandated three percent and from whom Hilaire had extorted another twenty-five percent.

One by one eleven more players stepped forward, forcing Cyrus and Hilaire to the center of a circle formed by huge, silent, glaring men, each of whom was perforated and made to look more menacing by dozens of tiny needles sticking out of him.

By this time, Hilaire was studying the placement of all those needles.

All Cyrus could do was look around fearfully, hold his palms up and say, "Guys, guys, guys, you're playin' with us, right. You sure put a good scare into Hilaire and me; we'll all have a good laugh about it and —"

"No," McGill said. He slipped between Matthew and another player into the circle. "Your clients are here to renegotiate their contracts, and get back the money you stole from them. Now, you can either agree to their demands or I'll call the U.S. attorney for the Eastern District of Louisiana and let you and the guys explain yourselves to her. If that doesn't scare you, Mr. Zale, I'll call the NFL office in New York, too."

"Who the hell are you, mister?" Zale asked. "And what've you done to all my boys?"

It amused McGill, and reassured him, when someone failed to recognize him.

Made him think there might be some measure of privacy for him after Patti left office.

"I'm the guy who figured out your scam, and the guy who will put you in federal prison, if you don't go along with the game plan. That's all you need to know."

"You're showing us your voodoo is stronger than mine," Hilaire said.

"It's called acupuncture, but yeah," McGill said. "We had a specialist come in to treat the guys, tell them stories about facing down enemies and they started feeling better right away. We've got a nice case of corresponding healing going on here. You use pins to hurt; we use needles to heal."

Hilaire smiled. "You're a pretty smart fella. Maybe you and me should talk."

That made Cyrus look at her and frown.

McGill told him, "Don't worry. I'm spoken for."

The moment of displeasure with Hilaire was enough to spark defiance in Cyrus.

He said to McGill, "So what if I don't like your game plan? What if I say you let me out of here or I'll file charges against *you?* False imprisonment or something like that."

"That would be a difficult charge to sustain," McGill said. "Because if you're not agreeable my friends and I will be the ones to leave the room, and you'll have some time to chat in private with your clients. I believe you saw the error of your ways when you spoke with Matthew. Now, the other guys can put a word in your ear, too."

As planned and diagrammed by McGill, the players tightened

the circle.

McGill could feel the aura of power the huge young men generated.

They weren't even ticked off at him but it was still intimidating.

Cyrus Zale's face turned to Jell-O. "Okay, okay, okay. What do you want?"

The players stepped back, as planned.

McGill said, "The first thing you have to understand is there will be no bargaining. You raise any objections, I step aside and you're on your own. You understand? Good. You terminate your agreements with *all* your clients, not just the ones in this room. In fact, you get out of professional sports altogether."

That almost brought a cry of protest from Zale.

But the players closed in again, on their own.

Talented athletes knew when to improvise.

Zale nodded vigorously. The guys stayed close to keep the pressure on.

"You repay all the money you and Hilaire extorted from them. You'll place the commission you received from each player into a numbered account. Once that's done, you'll make sure you never contact them again, in person or by proxy. You do those things and you'll be free to find a new path in life. I'd ask you if that sounds good to you, but your opinion doesn't really matter here. Nod again if you understand."

Zale did, and he raised his hand.

"What?" McGill asked.

"What about her?" he said, inclining his head Hilaire's way.

"We're going to talk with her after we're done with you."

They were done with Zale in short order. McGill had brought forms for him to sign for each player, releasing them from their contracts with him and acknowledging the amount of money he owed each of them. Collecting those sums wouldn't be easy, but McGill had one idea that might help.

Before Zale left the room, Sweetie tossed a fetish to McGill.

It looked just like Zale.

"Maybe you don't believe in voodoo," McGill said, "but if you don't make good on your repayments, maybe you'll find a reason to change your mind."

McGill handed the doll to Hilaire.

She smiled. Zale glared at her, but left while he could.

Deke closed the door behind him.

McGill told Hilaire, "Matthew has said he'd be willing to pay you a three percent commission to represent his interests. You still feel that way, Matthew?"

The young giant nodded. Hilaire smiled at him.

The other players took notice.

"You guys all need a new agent. Don't feel obligated to make the same decision Matthew did, but, who knows, maybe Hilaire could work some good juju for all your careers."

Hilaire gave McGill her best smile; it was damn near bewitching.

Didn't keep him from telling her, "I'll be watching to make sure everyone's best interests are represented."

On the way out of the room, McGill noticed Hilaire talking not with any of her new clients but with J. R. Sullivan. Two pros at the insertion and removal of pointed objects. McGill might have been concerned for the guy if he hadn't tested his mettle under fire.

On the flight home, Sweetie told McGill, "That wrapped up nicely."

He said, "If it wasn't corny, I'd say neat as a pin."

"But you said it anyway."

"Yeah."

"You're not worried about a voodoo queen helping all those guys play against the Bears?"

McGill laughed. "No, I was worried about hanging around her too long."

Leaving no room for misunderstanding, he added, "I was tempted to ask Hilaire if she could bring Vince Lombardi back from the dead to coach our guys this time."

Sweetie loved the idea.

About the Author

Joseph Flynn has been published both traditionally — Signet Books, Bantam Books and Variance Publishing — and through his own imprint, Stray Dog Press, Inc. Both major media reviews and reader reviews have praised his work. Booklist said, "Flynn is an excellent storyteller." The Chicago Tribune said, "Flynn [is] a master of high-octane plotting." The most repeated reader comment is: Write faster, we want more.

Contact Joe at Hey Joe on his website: *www.josephflynn.com*

All of Joe's books are available for the Kindle or free Kindle app through www.amazon.com.

The Jim McGill Series
The President's Henchman, A Jim McGill Novel [#1]
The Hangman's Companion, A JimMcGill Novel [#2]
The K Street Killer A JimMcGill Novel [#3]
Part 1: The Last Ballot Cast, A JimMcGill Novel [#4 Part 1]
Part 2: The Last Ballot Cast, A JimMcGill Novel [#4 Part 2]
The Devil on the Doorstep, A Jim McGill Novel [#5]
The Good Guy with a Gun, A Jim McGill Novel [#6]
The Echo of the Whip, A Jim McGill Novel [#7]
McGill's Short Cases 1-3

The Ron Ketchum Mystery Series
Nailed, A Ron Ketchum Mystery [#1]
Defiled, A Ron Ketchum Mystery Featuring John Tall Wolf [#2]
Impaled, A Ron Ketchum Mystery [#3]

The John Tall Wolf Series
Tall Man in Ray-Bans, A John Tall Wolf Novel [#1]
War Party, A John Tall Wolf Novel [#2]
Super Chief, a John Tall Wolf Novel [#3]
Smoke Signals, a John Tall Wolf Novel [#4]

The Zeke Edison Series
Kill Me Twice [#1]

Stand Alone Titles
The Concrete Inquisition
Digger
The Next President
Hot Type
Farewell Performance
Gasoline, Texas
Round Robin, A Love Story of Epic Proportions
One False Step
Blood Street Punx
Still Coming
Still Coming Expanded Edition
Hangman — A Western Novella
Pointy Teeth: Twelve Bite-Sized Stories

You may read free excerpts of Joe's books by visiting his website at: www.josephflynn.com.